Don't Pass the Exits

Copyright@ Mike Hourston

This is a work of fiction. Names, characters, and incidents depicted in these stories are products of the author's imagination and are used fictitiously. Any resemblance to actual events, or persons living or dead, is entirely coincidental and beyond the intent of the author.

ISBN: 9798376802847

"A room without books is like a body without a soul."

Cicero

Contents

Can Truth Be Told?	1
The Ironton Exit	66
Lost and Found in Glasgow	75
Next Stop Wunderland	93
A Story Worth Telling	107
Six Blocks Down	124
What about Bonnie?	133
Shadows in the Maelstrom	136

Can Truth Be Told?

"I was dead once," Sean said.

Phil swung around on the barstool. "Come again?"

"I died a few weeks ago."

"How much you been drinking?"

"I ain't drunk!"

"Then what are you doing in a dump like the Green Tavern?"

"They said to come here."

Janet, clutching a half-empty glass of beer, leaned toward Sean. "Who the hell are 'they'?"

"Spirits you face when you die."

Phil laughed. "Were these good or bad spirits?"

"The damned can't come back. I'm here, so they had to be on the side of good."

Phil grabbed Sean by the arm. "Let's get a table and you can tell me all about your death and these spirits."

Sean pulled away. "I'm serious. And I got a job to do."

"Alright, let's hear your story. Maybe we can get you help."

Janet stumbled off her barstool and followed Phil and Sean to a table in the back.

The Green Tavern, at the corner of Tucker and Grand, had been a neighborhood fixture since 1935. These days, even on Saturday night, you'd never see more than ten or twelve people there. It was old, rundown, and ignored—like the neighborhood.

Phil helped seat Janet, and then signaled Craig the bartender to bring over three beers.

Sean Kelly, a freckle-faced redhead in white shirt and black slacks, stood a muscular six feet. He'd graduated from an Ivy League university and was a rising star at the prestigious Maxim and Sons architectural firm. Tall and thin, Phil Serling was in his early forties. A good athlete in high school, he'd gotten a basketball scholarship to State University. He left school after injuring his knee as a freshman. Since then, he'd worked at factory, warehouse, and delivery jobs in the neighborhood. He'd been unemployed the last six months. Janet Powers, a blue-eyed overweight blonde, got married at sixteen. Thrice divorced, she admitted to being fifty-two.

They introduced themselves, and then Phil leaned back in his chair. "Tell me about your visit to the other side…and this job you got to do."

Sean slung his tan sports jacket over the back of his chair and glanced out the window as a car sped by. "A few weeks ago, I'd just turned thirty and decided to treat myself to a day of fishing over at Spanish Lake. Alone in a canoe, I did more drinking than fishing."

Janet interrupted. "I hate drinking alone."

The bartender brought over the beers and a basket of pretzels, and then tossed Phil some keys. "It's after one o'clock and the place is empty besides you guys. I'm heading home. Do me a favor and lock up."

The only things new at the Green Tavern were six red-cushioned bar stools. Half its ceiling fans didn't work, and wooden tables and chairs were worn—most wobbled. Much of the gray-tiled floor was scuffed raw to the wood. When walked on, the old floor planks gave off a cracking sound.

Phil reached into his shirt pocket for a cigarette. "Go on with your story."

"The canoe flipped over. Cold water filled my nose and mouth—I couldn't breathe. And then I'm somewhere else." He gripped the beer mug. "I'm standing next to this tree—everything's dark. Beams of bright-yellow light come at me wrapped in a kind of cloudy mist. Funny, I didn't feel scared. Right in front of me are two glowing figures. They hover for a moment and then ask me to go back to help secure truth and address an injustice."

"I thought the next world rewarded good and punished evil. Whatever it is, it'll come to them in good time."

"I didn't ask why they wouldn't wait."

"What makes you so damn special that they sent you on this mission?"

Sean shrugged as the wind picked up and it began to rain. "I don't know. I've tried to live an honest life with respect for truth and others. Nothing special—that's everyone's job."

"Maybe that's all it takes," Janet quipped.

Sean raised his voice. "They asked and here I am! I wasn't going to argue."

Phil leaned across the table. "What are you supposed to do?"

Someone began knocking at the front door. As the pounding got louder, Phil yelled, "The place is closed."

When the knocks continued, Phil said, "Get lost, or I'll call the cops."

A few seconds later, two lean figures, standing in the pouring rain, stared at them through the window.

Startled, Janet said, "Who the hell are they?"

Phil shook his head. "Looks like a couple of neighborhood bums. There's a lot of them around here."

Sean studied the men's exhausted faces. "Let them in. They're gonna be a part of this."

"Be a part of what?" Phil yelled.

Phil hesitated, and then walked over to the bar and reached under the counter—pulling out a .38 pistol. He glanced at Sean as he unlocked the door. "This is dumb." As the men entered, Phil pointed to the carpet as he waved his gun. "Wipe your feet, and don't try anything."

Neither had socks and their tennis shoes were worn and ripped in spots. Both had several days' worth of beard and wore the same style red-and-yellow plaid shirt. Their sunken faces, skinny frames, and pale complexions suggested neither had eaten much in a while.

Phil grabbed a dirty green towel from behind the bar and tossed it at them. "Use this and then grab a seat over there. I'll get you guys something to drink." He looked at Sean. "He's buying. You guys can stay till the rain slows down."

Phil handed each a beer. "Don't get rowdy, or I'll toss you out on your asses."

Janet shoved the basket of pretzels. "Try these—they're good."

The men introduced themselves as Kevin Cleve and Andy Jakowski. Both claimed to be in their forties but looked twenty years older. They shared a tent in a homeless village about six blocks from the Green Tavern.

"What were you guys doing out there?" Janet asked.

Kevin, his teeth stained bright yellow, smiled. "Just scrounging around, you never know what you might find. We work this neighborhood on a regular basis, everybody else goes downtown. Last week, Andy found an unopened bottle of wine, and I came across a pair of insulated rubber boots in an abandoned house just down the street. They'll be handy when the weather gets cold."

"We've talked about relocating up here. There's a place just around the corner that's move-in ready," Andy said.

"A couple of cats live there now. We've named them Gertrude and Molly, and don't think they'd mind sharing the place," Kevin added.

Phil shook his head as he turned to Sean. "Where'd you leave off?"

"Like I said, these two spirits asked me to come back to secure truth and see if justice follows."

"How you gonna do that?"

"Expose Mayor Joe Delancey and his son Little Joe for a crime and cover-up."

Phil jumped up from his chair. "Are you kidding? Delancey has influence with big business, big media, and big government. And his political party stands by him no matter what he does. Some folks are above the law, and he's one of them. I agreed to listen, but not to commit suicide. Hell, your whole story is crazy—I died and came back. Where's the proof for any of this bullshit?"

"The ambulance workers said I didn't have a pulse. The doctors at the hospital reported me dead—even threw a sheet over my head. I did meet two spirits!"

"Hell—that shit happens all the time. People ain't dead, they're just dreaming. I ain't risking my neck over your imagination." He pointed upward. "Have them spirits show us something."

Phil took a drag on his cigarette and then glanced at Kevin and Andy. "Finish your drinks and take the pretzels with you."

Janet slapped the table. "I wanna help."

Kevin and Andy raised their glasses. "We'll join in."

"That's booze talk. Tomorrow you fools will forget you were even here," Phil said.

Phil faced Sean. "You say spirits are behind this. Have them spin the table around or make it rise off the floor."

Sean sat quiet for a few seconds, hands covering his face. A gust of wind shoved the tavern door open, and rain poured in. Lights flickered and the jukebox began to softly play an old country ballad.

Phil ran over and slammed the door, and then pulled the electrical cord out from the jukebox.

"I'm sure I saw two beams of light near the bar," Kevin said.

Andy nodded. "I did too."

Sean held two twenties as he glanced at Phil standing near the bar. "Grab a couple bottles of their best brandy. It's on me."

Phil shrugged. "Why not—as long as you're paying for this party."

Sean signaled Andy and Kevin to scoot their chairs closer. "What am I doing here? What are we doing here?" He took a drink, and then glanced around the table. "A few weeks ago, every day looked the same—and then I died. Dying wakes you to the meaning of life. That's the reason I'm back. A beautiful twenty-year-old woman named Cathy Mason got murdered—and we're doing something about it."

Sean reached into his coat pocket and handed everyone a small photo.

"What a lovely gal. And look at that smile," Janet said.

"She was beaten to death outside her apartment. The mayor's people got a seventeen year-old delivery boy to confess to the crime. The prosecutor declared the crime solved. The kid's public attorney is working on a plea deal with the prosecutors. But the kid didn't do it. Little Joe Delancey, the mayor's son, killed her."

"The spirits told you all this?" Janet asked.

"They told me Cathy Mason was murdered, and Little Joe did it. The rest I researched since coming back."

"Why don't the spirits just wave their wand and make everything right?" Janet asked.

"That's not the way it works. When asked, they'll help us here and there. But a just world is mankind's challenge—always has been. Our job will be to gather truth and share it. What happens next is up to this world."

"Are her parents going to help with this?" Kevin wondered.

"They're dead."

Sean brushed back his red hair. "Are you guys ready to get this started?"

Everyone agreed, and then Sean pointed at Phil and Janet. "You two check on the mayor's political associates—people brag about things they get away with. That's a lot of ground, but we might uncover information we can leverage against him or some of his friends."

Sean turned to Kevin and Andy. "You guys talk to people on the street that might have seen or heard something.

"And I'll look for a money trail. Cover-ups cost money or favors done in return. Maybe I can crack the money foundation around him by exposing financial misdeeds. Get folks running for cover and somebody might be willing to throw the mayor under the bus." He paused for a second. "Sooner or later, we're going to have a bunch of powerful people angry at us. And we know they're dangerous. Does anyone want to back out of this?"

Janet raised her hand. "What about pay? I want to help, but I got bills."

"Me too," Phil added.

"I'll give you five-hundred dollars a week, payable when we get together here for our weekly updates. Let's make that Friday evenings, around six o'clock." Sean added, "I'm paying for results, not to keep you guys in booze or drugs. I expect you to earn the money."

"Do we each get five hundred, or do we have to split it?" Kevin asked.

"You get five-hundred apiece, but your effort has to produce something. I know you can do it. The spirits have brought us together for a reason."

"What about expenses?" Janet asked.

"Call me if you need cash to buy information, or anything else."

Phil glanced at Sean. "For five-hundred bucks a week, I'll give it a shot for a while."

Andy looked around the room, and then at Sean. "Those spirits—have they got names?"

"Of course, but for now spirits will do."

After Sean refilled everyone's glass, they spent the next few hours figuring where to start their respective investigations. Sean would keep the records, documents, and information they'd use to build their case.

Sean shared his phone number and insisted they contact him anytime circumstances dictated, and then handed everyone five hundred dollars to get started.

The rain had stopped, and sunlight was poking through the clouds when Sean checked his watch. "It's five-thirty, time to head home." He turned to Kevin and Andy. "Do you guys need a ride back to your camp?"

"Could you drop us off at Harry's Food Shelter, over on Highland Avenue? Sunday mornings they serve a special pancake breakfast," Kevin said.

"No problem."

Janet sang as she headed to a bus stop around the corner.

Phil locked the place, dropped the keys in a flowerpot near the door, and then jumped in his old rusty green Mercury Sable.

After dropping off Kevin and Andy at the food shelter, Sean sat in his Mercedes wondering if the team he'd assembled would be up to the challenge of delivering truth about Cathy Mason's murder.

The forces aligned against this challenge were powerful. But, the spirits sent him to the Green Tavern and this is the team he got. He'd let it go at that.

Monday morning was sunny and seventy degrees as Sean parked near the offices of brokerage giant XL and Company. Trillions in financial assets flowed through those forty-five floors of concrete, steel, glass, and computer hardware. Fred Buckley, a friend of Sean's from college days, was their chief accountant.

The elevator opened on the 40th floor, and Sean followed a group of well-dressed men through glass doors into a lounge-like space with sofas, large, cushioned chairs, and several big screen televisions.

He approached the attractive young receptionist. "I've got a nine o'clock appointment with Mr. Buckley. Tell him Sean Kelley is here."

She pointed. "His office is down the hall third on the right—he's waiting."

Sean rounded the corner passing bold shades of red, green, and yellow framing the walls leading to Fred's office.

Sean thrust out his right hand. "I see you guys favor Impressionists."

Fred, in a blue pin-stripe suit, nodded. "That's what the top floor likes, so that's what we buy. There's over ten million bucks hanging on the walls out there." He walked to a portable bar in the office and held up a bottle. "Is apricot brandy still your drink of choice?"

"Yep—pour me a short one."

Fred handed Sean his drink as they sat on the black-leather couch. "I heard about your accident. How are you doing? You look OK."

"I spent two weeks in the hospital fighting a lung infection. I've recovered but am taking time off to get some things done. I've been given a three-month paid leave of absence."

"That's generous. Do you still live at the Artemis Avenue Apartments?"

"Yep."

"Best place in the city. I can't afford it—yet."

Sean surveyed the room. "You're sure moving up in the world. A few years ago, you were buried in a cubby hole thirty floors down. What's your secret?"

Fred leaned back on the couch and raised his glass. "It's all about knowing people worth knowing. Doing favors and getting favors. That's the talent that counts these days."

Sean laughed, and said, "Would you have time to do an old college buddy a big favor?"

"What's the deal?"

"I need you to research Mayor Joe Delancey and his son Little Joe. Get all the financial dirt you can dig up on him no matter where it leads."

"Wow—that dude is heavy. Why are you looking into him?"

"A couple of superheavyweights have requested it."

"Can you drop their names?"

"Not now, but they're worth knowing. They're the best networking partners you'll ever have. Trust me—they'll appreciate your help."

Fred thought a moment. "Sounds good—I'd like to add that kind of weight to my network. I can start overseas; I got contacts in Switzerland, the Bahamas, and in China. I'll call you when I get my hands on something you can use. This might take a while; the mayor has got his fingers everywhere."

"Do what you can. You'll be on the right side of things."

"I just want to be on the winning side of things—that's all that counts." Fred set his empty glass on the coffee table. "By the way, Delancey and his chief of staff, a guy named Franklin, have nasty reputations for rough stuff. Can your friends promise us cover?"

"Be discreet. But don't worry; things work out in the long run. And if you come across the name Cathy Mason—see where that leads. She's part of this."

"What's her role?"

"She's one of their victims."

Fred jotted her name. "I'll get started this afternoon. Remember to tell your friends how much I helped."

"They'll know. In the future, let's meet at Harvey's Bar & Grill over on Belmont Street."

"Sounds good, they serve a great steak and got quiet tables in the back."

A middle-aged, slightly bent, gray-haired man waved as he walked past Fred's office.

Fred grinned at Sean. "That's what a loser looks like. He's never got past the sixth floor—except to deliver stuff. In six months, he'll be on the street."

"What's wrong with him?"

"With losers—who knows. It could be anything, or nothing. The world is full of guys just like that." He glanced upward. "I plan to be on the top floor by the time I'm thirty-five. Better views, more power, and much better pay."

He walked Sean to the elevator, and then headed back to his office to make a few calls.

Monday afternoon, Phil wondered about his commitment to Sean's project while he finished a juicy fat burger at Spanky's. He didn't buy the spirits, but the money sounded good so he figured to stretch things as far as he could until things got dangerous. After lunch, he called Janet and told her he'd drop by to discuss the project.

On the way over, Phil spotted Andy and Kevin pushing a screeching metal shopping cart piled with clothes, plastic containers, and other goods.

He pulled to the curb, and yelled, "Where are you guys heading?"

"We're moving to new digs, been thinking about it for a while. A guy at the camp got beat up over a slice of fruitcake this morning," Andy said.

"We're going to share a place with a couple of cats. You remember," Kevin said.

"I thought you were kidding about those cats."

"Oh, no, Gertrude and Molly are very sweet—and smart. And with this money coming in, the four of us should be fine," Kevin said.

Phil leaned out the car window. "Remember, you got to earn the money."

"We will, and the cats have agreed to help," Andy said.

"That should be interesting. But why not—everything else about this is strange. Can I give you a hand?"

Andy pushed the cart. "No, we're good. Tomorrow we'll see what the street knows about this murder."

"Hey, what's with those books on the bottom of the cart?"

"They're Andy's books. Every Sunday at the camp he reads passages and quotes from Aristotle or Socrates or recites poetry like Keats' *Ode to a Nightingale*. Everybody loves Keats."

Phil waved as he drove off. "Grease those wheels—I heard you guys a block away."

Five minutes later, Phil parked on a street lined with once grand two-story brick homes from the 1890s. According to his grandmother, the Walnut Park neighborhood once had a streetcar line running past fancy restaurants and big department stores. Saint Jerome's church, long closed, had been packed every Sunday, its grade school considered the best in the city. She told him about the neighborhood's sweet spring and summer smells from gardens bursting with red and yellow roses and golden honeysuckle. And she claimed people were always well-dressed, polite, and generous.

Phil surveyed the splattered chunks of glass and big potholes in front of Janet's home. Yards were patches of weeds strewn with rusty car parts and discarded hot-water heaters. Bricks showed wear, and all had faded to a sunbaked light tan. Windows were either boarded or had metal bars. Roof tiles lay everywhere.

Phil beat on the steel door as a group of loud-talking teenage boys strolled past his car. A rotten eggs odor blanketed the area.

Janet poked her head out the second-story window. "I'll be right down."

The boys continued down the street as Janet opened the door.

"I keep this locked all the time," Janet said.

Phil held his nose. "What's that stink?"

"See it, a couple of yards over. Under that swarm of flies a dead dog's been baking in this heat for three days. She was a golden retriever named Clara. Don't know what happened. I called a couple of times, but the city hasn't bothered to clean it up."

"No way to end—even for a dog."

Janet shrugged. "Come on in."

The worn wood banister wobbled as Phil climbed the stairs.

"Careful," Janet said.

"You need to get that fixed."

"I ain't got the money. The air conditioner went out a couple of years ago, and I have trouble paying my heating bills. When you're broke, things around you get broke and stay broke. I use two sweaters to keep out the cold. Summer heat is relentless—I drip all day and lay in a pool of stinking sweat at night."

At the top of the stairs, Janet drew Phil's attention to the two-story foyer. "They say there used to be a giant crystal chandelier hanging there brightening the house at night. People saw the light from blocks away. It was grand around here—they say."

Phil glanced at the torn carpet and peeling light-green wallpaper. "When you're down—old times and old dreams is all you got."

They entered a small room crammed tight with a couple of easy chairs, a worn gray cloth couch covered in stains, a scratched wooden coffee table, and two floor lamps. Thick dust and grime covered the solid oak flooring. The ten-foot ceiling's white plaster showed large cracks and big streaks where water leaked through.

Janet brushed a few popcorn kernels off the couch as she plopped down. "Where do we start?"

"Mind if I smoke?"

"Toss me one."

Phil glanced out the window. "Let's hang around city hall and listen for loose talk. If we pick up anything good, we go from there."

"We can't just walk in—they got security. You have to show you got a reason for being there. You got to know somebody, have business with the mayor or someone with his machine."

"We don't need to get inside city hall. There are all kinds of restaurants, coffee shops, outdoor cafes, and bars around there. We scout around; find out where some of the movers and shakers hang out."

"Who are these people we want to follow around?"

"We start with the mayor's office website. It lists his entire staff, with photos. I'll bet everyone on his staff has juicy stories."

"That's great, but how are we going to get them to share with us. We're nobody."

"Hell, I ain't got all the answers. Let's do the research, and then figure out the rest."

Janet took one last drag and then dropped the butt in a glass cup next to the couch. "I ain't got a computer, and don't know how to use one."

"We'll go to the library, they've plenty. I'm not a wiz but can navigate the Internet. Don't worry, the research will be easy."

"Hanging in those restaurants and bars will be expensive. Do you think Sean will pop for all that?"

"He's got plenty of money—you can tell. Did you notice his clothes? And he drove up in a new Mercedes."

"I've been thinking about those spirits. How much do you think they'll help us?"

"I wouldn't worry about them. Let's just see how much money we can pull out of this."

Janet glanced at the photograph of the murdered girl. "I would like to do something for Cathy."

"There's nothing wrong with helping ourselves at the same time. Besides, spirits ain't against people making money."

Janet eased herself off the couch and borrowed another cigarette. "I don't know—maybe you're right. I could use a few things."

"I'll pick you up tomorrow around ten o'clock and we'll head over to the library on Jefferson."

Janet nodded. "I'll need some outfits, and at least two new pair of shoes." She looked in the mirror. "The gray is leaking through. I need to have my hair fixed before we go anywhere."

Phil laughed as he headed toward the door. "Come to think of it—I could use a couple of suits."

Kevin and Andy still had good friends back at the homeless encampment, but they'd been looking for new digs for a while. The money from Sean would make the transition easier.

"That's the last of it. Where do you want to store the shopping cart?" Andy asked.

"Shove it right behind the front door. That way we'll hear anyone trying to break in at night," Kevin said.

Built in 1903, the three-thousand square foot single-story frame building had served as a post office for over fifty years. Long abandoned, its flat tarred roof had a few leaks. The siding had shed a few of its gray shingles. But the thick block glass windows were intact, and the concrete floor in good shape. For twenty dollars a week a gas station attendant down the block agreed to give Kevin and Andy access to the restroom at night..

Andy looked up and down the street. "We were lucky to get this place before someone else scooped it up."

Kevin slapped his hands together. "It has so much potential. And with all the money coming in we'll fix it up and have friends over."

"Tomorrow we'll ask around the camp about that girl's death. Let's start with Jacob—he used to be a security guard and still knows folks on the police force."

"It'll be the first time in years I'll be doing something worthwhile."

Andy rolled a small plastic ball toward the cats. "Same here—and it feels good."

The Artemis Avenue Apartments, now converted to condos, were among the most expensive properties in the city. Surrounded by parks, theaters, retail, and the city's best restaurants, it's where the wealthy lived, or wished to live. Sean inherited his Number 10, Artemis Avenue residence from his parents.

Tuesday morning, Sean exited the elevator in jeans and red short-sleeve sport shirt. He said a quick hello to the doorman Charles and headed down Eighth Avenue, greeted by its smells of fresh-baked pastries, bacon on the griddle, and coffee brewing.

Choices were endless, but this morning the sugary aroma from Katz's Bakery proved too much. Sean grabbed a booth by the window and ordered three eclairs and coffee. Fifteen minutes later, he licked a piece of chocolate off his fingertips as he studied passing foot traffic. Two middle-aged men in gray tuxedos yelled and waved their arms as they rushed by. Right behind them, a thin gray-haired woman, at least in her sixties, dragged a noisy white poodle on a short black leash. A cabbie slammed on his brakes and cursed at teenagers slow walking across the street. They laughed and fingered him back. And so, it went.

Around ten-thirty, Sean arrived at the *Time's Building*. The paper had published a brief back-page story about the Cathy Mason murder and the kid arrested. The byline belonged to a woman named Charlene Grossman. Sean had called her and implied he was an old boyfriend of Cathy's, and she agreed to meet him in the lobby. She'd be standing next to the vending machines.

Sean held the glass door for a well-dressed elderly couple, and followed them inside where he got bumped and jostled while scanning the busy bright lobby. He spotted a tall, slim brunette holding a white-plastic cup with a gold purse slung over her shoulder.

Sean walked up. "Are you Charlene Grossman?"

She tossed the cup into a waste can. "You must be Sean. Let's head outside."

Sean rubbed his arm as they exited. "A lot of sharp elbows in there."

"Get in their way and they'll knock you over."

"Why do people put up with that kind of behavior?"

"Cause those folks got power and everybody knows it." She reached in her purse for a cigarette. "You said on the phone you had been close to the murdered girl, Cathy."

"We dated a while back, and I just heard about her tragic death. Your paper covered the story. I came to town to see if I could run down more details."

"Let's grab a bench and talk." After they were seated, she held up a cigarette. "Give me a light."

"Sure."

After a long drag, she said, "What kind of bullshit are you trying to run by me? I smell a con a mile away. What's this about?"

"All right—the truth. Her death troubles me, and I know there's a lot about the story that hasn't come out."

"Why the hell do you care?"

"Somebody should care about a miscarriage of justice. Talk about bullshit, that kid didn't kill her."

"You know it for a fact?"

"I do!"

Charlene looked away. "So do I, but there ain't a damn thing I can do about it."

"Can't, or won't?"

"Either way—it doesn't matter. The story I wrote is the one they'll let me write."

"Who are they?"

"The folks we talked about—the one's with power."

They sat silent for a moment, and then Sean said, "Will you help me secure the truth about this?"

"I don't know who you are, but you need to climb down from that cloud you're floating on before you get hurt—or get somebody else hurt." She inched closer. "God damn, what the hell are truth and justice anyway. They're just fucking words the powerful use to control. Don't make more of it. And never risk your ass over it."

"They may be twisted these days, but they're never meaningless words. I'm going to expose those responsible for Cathy's murder and cover-up."

"Let's say that happens. Nobody's going to do anything about it."

"We'll see."

Charlene glanced down the block. "I gotta get back to the office."

"Can I call you?"

"No—never."

When they got to the *Times Building*, Charlene grabbed Sean by the arm. "Talk to Mary Pence. She lived the next apartment over from Cathy. But don't mention my name."

Sean yelled thanks as Charlene disappeared inside.

On the ride home, Sean searched the Internet for a Mary Pence. An obituary from 1950 pulled up, and someone that lived in California. But no local hits under that name. He decided to drive to the Riverwood Apartments the next morning to see if he could get an interview.

Around two-thirty Sean's phone rang—it was Phil.

"Yes, Phil, what can I do for you?"

"Me and Janet came up with names of people on the mayor's staff. Plans are to follow them to where they do lunch and dinner around the mayor's office, and see if we can strike up conversations, maybe pick up some useful information."

"That sounds good."

"But it's expensive around there. Those restaurants and bars ain't cheap, and we can't show up in rags. They wouldn't let us in."

"What do you need?"

"We figure a grand each for clothes and walking-around money—to get us started. We got to look like we fit in."

"OK but remember I'm paying for results. That's means useful information that ties to Cathy's murder and cover-up."

"We know."

"I'll meet you at the Tavern in an hour."

Gertrude and Molly came running as Andy scraped a can of soft cat food on a couple of white plastic plates.

Kevin looked over as he shoved the metal cart away from the door. "Let's get going."

"I'm ready."

Andy checked his new wristwatch as they headed down the street. "It's eight-thirty; if we hurry, we can get to the camp by nine."

"We need a lock for the front door," Kevin said.

"Plus, furniture; I know a second-hand store that has decent tables and chairs."

After cutting through a couple of vacant lots, they climbed a small backyard chain-link fence where they encountered a growling bulldog that chased them out the gate.

After outrunning the dog, Kevin bent over. "Give me a minute to catch my breath. Hell, that fat old dog chomped at my heels all the way up the alley. These knees ain't made for running anymore." He eased himself to the curb, and said, "I've been thinking about Sean's spirits. Rich or poor, there's a day of reckoning for all this."

"I've always prayed—every night. It's no accident all of us showed up at the Tavern—those spirits brought us together."

"No matter the risk, let's see this through."

Andy helped Kevin up from the curb. "You cut yourself."

Kevin rubbed his hand. "Yeah, it happened when I jumped over that fence. It'll be OK."

Andy glanced at the camp. "We'll start by talking with Jacob. He spent eighteen years in the security business, and still has a lot of cop friends."

"He's a great guy—he'll help."

At the corner, they passed a line leading from Bob's Bakery truck where a young man handed out free day-old glazed and jelly donuts.

Founded ten years earlier by a homeless couple named Abe and Jenny Schmidt, the camp included various-sized tents, sleeping bags, and cardboard boxes spread over a couple of old parking lots in a rundown section of town covering some five acres. On weekdays the residents numbered three to four hundred, which could double on weekends. There were always large numbers of transients stopping for a few days or so. A couple of drinking fountains in the park across the street provided fresh water. A local charity contributed half a dozen porta potties and large metal trash containers. Abe Schmidt passed away a couple of years earlier at the age of seventy-nine. Jenny—called Mother Schmidt by everyone—still lived at the camp.

Andy pointed at a pair of scab-covered feet protruding from a tent. "It didn't take long for someone to grab our spot."

Kevin glanced at the plastic wrappers and cups, paper bags, and discarded needles. "They're welcome to it and the rest of this place."

They spotted Jacob across the street relaxed on a bench smoking a cigarette. Andy waved as they approached.

Jacob, in jeans and dirty gray sweatshirt, extended his hand. "I heard you guys moved out. Did you show up for donut day?"

Kevin laughed. "No, we're done with this—don't need it. We buy our own donuts these days."

Jacob rubbed his chin. "What I need is a shave. I'm getting tired or just lazy these days."

Andy pointed at Jacob's shiny brown leather shoes. "They always look great—you're quite the man-about-town."

"I polish my shoes first thing every morning. It makes me feel like I got someplace important to go."

"I understand."

"We got a permanent place about six blocks from here. And money coming in—we're working. That's why we're here," Kevin said.

Jacob dropped his cigarette, grabbed his chest, coughed for half a minute, and then picked up the still smoldering butt.

Andy rested his hand on Jacob's shoulder. "You need to quit those, and have that clinic check your cough."

"I've been to the clinic. I'm fifty and they tell me I won't see fifty-one." He leaned back on the bench and took a drag. "You said you're working. What's the deal?"

Andy began, "I'm so sorry."

Jacob raised his hand. "Things are what they are."

"OK. Have you heard the name Cathy Mason? She got murdered a few weeks back and they're claiming a delivery boy did the killing."

"I've never heard of her. Why?"

"We know for a fact that's not the way it happened," Andy said.

"And we're going to prove it," Kevin added.

"How do you know that?"

"A guy told us—and we believe him," Andy said.

"Did he show evidence?"

"You had to be there—at the Green Tavern. We're convinced the mayor's son did the murder, and it's been covered up. We're getting cash money to dig up evidence," Andy said.

Jacob pulled a white rag from his pocket and dusted his shoes. "What can I do to help?"

Kevin leaned closer. "You have cop friends. We thought you could ask what they might have heard or seen. A cover-up this big has got to involve a bunch of folks. Figure framing the kid, hiding evidence, writing fake reports, and just looking the other way. There must be some honest folks down there that don't go for that shit."

"I hate the mayor—the fucker got me fired from my last job. I'd be happy to take that bastard and his kin down. I'll check with my buddies on the force and a guy I know at city hall."

Kevin handed Jacob a photo. "That's her."

"Very pretty."

Andy gave him two twenty-dollar bills. "This will get you started."

Jacob shoved the money in his pants pocket. "Don't flash that around here. You guys know better."

Kevin scratched their new address on a discarded match folder. "If we ain't there, just push your way in and wait—there's no lock. And you can keep the photo, we got another."

Jacob got up, coughed a couple of times, and lit a cigarette. "I'll start today. What are your plans?"

"We'll show the picture around the camp," Andy said.

While they talked, a group of twenty or so men and women walked past. One guy held a shovel, and another carried a small plastic bag.

"What are they burying?" Kevin asked.

Jacob shook his head. "That big gray squirrel living in the oak tree got run over last night. The car didn't even stop to check—the bastards."

Andy glanced over. "I remember when he first showed up at the camp. He loved rooting through trash bags. His favorite food was pecans."

As they began to dig, Jacob said, "I gotta get over there. I'm supposed to say a few words." He walked about ten feet and then looked back. "It's a damn shame—I'm gonna miss that squirrel."

Andy and Kevin spent an hour asking around the camp—with no luck. Before leaving, they said hello to Mother Schmidt. On the way home they bought a couple of shirts at the thrift store.

"It's six o'clock," Sean said.

Kevin glanced at the door. "Where are the others?"

"We'll give them a few minutes."

Sean sipped his beer, and then opened a briefcase, retrieving two small phones. "One for each of you—they're burner phones. It makes it easier for us to stay in touch. When you run out of minutes, I'll get you more."

Just then, Phil, in a dark-gray suit, white shirt and red tie, walked in. Janet followed in a black cotton dress, bright white shoes, with a large red purse—its strap slung over her shoulder.

"That's something," Sean said.

Andy held the chair as Janet approached. "Please have a seat."

Sean waved to the bartender, and then looked at Phil. "Do you guys still touch this cheap liquor?"

"Why not?"

Andy smiled, and said, "Madam, your hair looks perfect."

She swept back a few white-blond strands from her forehead. "I had to sit for two hours before she got the color just right. Next time I'm asking for a different girl."

After the beers arrived, Sean pointed at Andy. "Did you find out anything we can use?"

"Nobody at the camp heard anything, but we got somebody checking to see what the cops know. He's honest and got a grudge against the mayor. I'm sure he'll be helpful."

Sean pulled out a notebook. "What's his name?"

"Jacob."

"Does Jacob come with a last name?"

Andy shrugged his shoulders. "It's always just been Jacob."

"I think its Mundy," Kevin said.

"When do you expect to hear back from him?"

"He didn't say for sure. But it shouldn't be more than a few days. He's got great contacts," Kevin said.

"Is there anything else?"

"We need more photos of Cathy? We'll post them around and say there's a reward for information. I'll put my burner number on there, and let you know if we get any hits," Andy said.

"That's a great idea. But be careful, we don't want to alert anyone we're looking into this. Call me before you agree to meet anyone who claims they got information. It could be a set-up."

Sean set the notebook down. "I've got an old college friend checking on the mayor's finances here and overseas. I'm sure there's something there—we just need to expose it."

Phil opened a silver cigarette case and lit a cigarette.

"Where'd you steal that?" Kevin laughed.

"I don't steal!"

"I'm just kidding."

Sean watched Phil shove the case back inside his jacket, and then tapped the table with his right hand. "I got a name—Mary Pence. She lived next door to Cathy at the apartment complex. I drove over there but saw a couple of guys hanging around in front. They must be worried about her. I've been trying to hunt up her telephone number. She's not on social media."

"Did she see something?" Janet asked.

"Must have, otherwise they wouldn't be so concerned. I gotta talk to her."

"Where'd you get her name?" Phil asked.

"A person working at the *Times*."

"Who was that?"

"She won't get involved."

Andy scooted his chair closer to the table. "I don't trust the *Times* or anybody working there. They're worse than phonies."

"We'll see."

A loud thud drew their attention to an old man who had fallen off his barstool. The bartender dragged him to a nearby table where he passed out.

Janet shook her head. "That's Pete, he's always falling—been doing it for years."

"He doesn't hurt anybody," Kevin said.

"He's better than a *Times*' phony. They do real harm," Andy added.

Sean turned to Phil. "What have you guys been doing?"

"We've identified key players on the mayor's staff and tracked where they lunch and dinner." Phil responded.

"And where they drink," Janet said.

Phil squeezed out his cigarette and dropped the butt in his empty glass. "The mayor's chief of staff loves to hang at a place called the White Fox. He's a tough-looking son-of-a bitch, and spends hours sitting at the bar, drinking, talking, and telling jokes.

If anybody knows the mayor's secrets—he does. Plans are to try and grab a couple of barstools near him."

"We'll get him talking and steer the conversation to this Cathy thing—and we'll record every word. We figure he'll say something we can use," Janet said.

Phil said, "We know where we can get small voice-activated recorders. They're five-hundred dollars apiece, and we'll need two. The guy at the radio shop on Vandeventer showed them to us."

"Think he'll open up about something that sensitive?" Sean asked.

"Trust me, if he knows about it—he'll brag about it."

Sean looked around. "Bars get noisy. You sure the recorders will be able to follow a conversation?"

Phil shrugged. "We won't know unless we try."

"I guess we got nothing to lose. Go ahead."

Sean handed everyone their weekly pay and promised Janet and Phil additional funds for the recorders, plus dining-out money. "Call me if anything comes up. Otherwise, I'll see you guys next week."

Phil and Janet hurried out the door.

When they reached Phil's car, Janet said, "Andy and Kevin stink—I could barely stand it."

"It's just once a week. The pay and dining-out money make up for it."

"Yeah—I guess."

Sean finished his beer, thanked Andy and Kevin for their efforts, and handed them another forty dollars for expenses tied to Jacob along with a half-dozen photos of the murdered girl.

"Maybe the spirits can get you in to see that lady—Mary Pence," Andy said.

Sean smiled. "It won't hurt to ask. By the way, you guys need a ride."

"Nah, we're going to get Pete home. The walk will do him good."

Kevin paid Pete's bar bill, and then he and Andy hoisted old Pete off the chair and slow walked him a couple of blocks home to his wife.

Sunday morning Kevin and Andy posted the photos of Cathy, offering a thousand-dollar reward for information, and then headed to the park next to the homeless camp where Andy spent part of the afternoon sharing Keats' wisdom to a small crowd. Later, after distributing boxes of free pizza to the camp, a dozen students from a nearby liberal arts college came over to listen.

Andy had just read *Ode on a Grecian Urn* when he spotted Jacob seated on a park bench waving. He thanked his audience, grabbed Kevin, and headed over to see what Jacob might have found.

On their way, one of the female students ran up and handed Andy twenty dollars. "I love the Romantics—that Keats. He understood the world and left us such wonderful gifts."

"What's your name?"

"Cybil."

Andy shoved the twenty in his shirt pocket. "Great poetry unlocks the world and takes you places movies, television, sports, and video games can't go. Never lose your appreciation of its power."

"I won't." She smiled and rejoined her friends.

Jacob coughed into his sleeve. "Cops get a call a young gal is getting beat up. She's dead by the time they arrive. Within a couple of minutes, they nab a suspect, covered in blood. The officers recognize the bastard as the mayor's son, and they call the mayor's people. Meanwhile this old lady from the next apartment over is yelling she seen it all. She's the one that called the cops—her name's Mary Pence."

Andy looked at Kevin. "Sean mentioned her."

Jacob lit a cigarette. "Around that time the mayor and his private goons showed up along with his chief of staff—a tough guy named Dave Franklin. They take over managing the crime scene, and won't let the homicide and CSI folks in."

"Wow," Kevin said.

Jacob rubbed some dust off his shoe. "Yeah, they won't let cops do their job anymore. Anyway, the mayor's people got the lady's cellphone, took her statement, and told her not to talk to anyone about it. They cleaned up the crime scene, framed a delivery boy, and it looks like the mayor's son gets a free murder."

"What about the media?" Andy asked.

Jacob pulled out the photo of the dead girl Andy had given him earlier and shook his head. "Folks in the media don't care. They're all part of the same club, and this poor gal didn't belong. One of the officers tried to post something about this on social media. It got taken down within minutes, and he got suspended. It's rotten everywhere you look."

"The price of principle is awful high these days," Kevin said.

Jacob flicked his cigarette in the air. "What principle? Show me where it exists."

When Jacob started to cough, Andy said, "Anything else, before we let you go?"

"Oh, yeah, a *Times* reporter got in to see this witness, Ms. Pence. They killed whatever story she planned to write, and since then got Ms. Pence under house arrest till they figure out what to do with her. Bottom-line—she's in grave danger. Whatever you do, make it fast."

Andy slipped twenty dollars in Jacob's shirt pocket. "Stay safe, partner."

Jacob took a heavy drag from his cigarette. "Stop kidding yourself. Safe's an illusion—always has been."

On the way home, Kevin phoned Sean and brought him up to date about Mary Pence and the danger she was in. They discussed ways to secure her safety, including places she might hide until they could get her evidence and testimony in front of the public.

Monday morning, Sean sat in the kitchen finishing his third cup of coffee figuring how he'd slip past the mayor's thugs to interview Ms. Pence and get her to safety. He came up with a simple plan. Walk up to them like he didn't have a care in the world, flash a fake ID, and claim he was there on the mayor's business. Maybe they'd let him pass until they could check it out. By then, he'd be getting Ms. Pence's story. Assuming she'd let him in and wanted to share. The plan had a lot of ifs and maybes, but he had to move now.

Around nine-fifteen, Sean headed to Mary's place on Tay Avenue. Thirty minutes later he parked in front of a liquor store just around the corner from the run-down apartments. Gripping an attaché case, he passed a couple of heavy-set women seated on a metal bench laughing while splitting a bottle of wine.

At the complex parking lot, he noticed a late model Jeep with its driver leaning forward, arms draped around the steering wheel. As he walked past, he spotted three others slumped against the seats motionless with several empty liquor bottles on the floor. A smoldering half-smoked cigarette lay on the parking lot next to the driver's side door. The four men were dressed in T-Shirts and jeans, had long beaded hair and none looked over twenty. One of the men in the back seat had a gun shoved inside his waistband.

Sean climbed a small flight of concrete steps leading to a courtyard. At the top of the stairs, he saw two well-dressed young men sitting on a bench about thirty feet from Mary's apartment. He walked over and flashed a detective badge insisting he'd been sent by the mayor to interrogate Ms. Pence—and was in a hurry. They examined his badge, looked at each other, and then waved him on.

Sean rang the doorbell and then knocked, glancing over, and smiling at the men a couple of times.

After a minute, a thin gray-haired woman cracked open the door. "What the hell do you want?"

"Ma'am, I'd like to get a statement from you about the murder of your neighbor—Cathy Mason."

"I told you guys what happened, and you still framed that kid."

Sean drew closer to the door and whispered. "I don't work for the mayor, I know the kid got framed, and I'm gonna make sure the truth gets out—with your help."

"Why—who are you?"

"My name is Sean Kelly, and I've made a commitment to expose those responsible for Cathy's murder and the cover-up."

"You made a commitment to whom?"

"To myself and others."

She opened the door a crack wider and stared at the men on the bench. "How'd you get past those two hoodlums?"

"They think I work for the mayor."

"Might as well hear what you got to say. Would you like a cup of coffee and a jellied sweet roll?"

"That sounds good."

Sean retrieved a video/audio recorder from his attaché case and held it up. "I want to use this to record everything. Is that OK?"

"That's fine. Take a seat on the couch."

A few minutes later, she handed Sean his drink, put a tray of raspberry rolls on the coffee table, and sat in a big brown easy chair.

She tossed Sean a napkin. "That jelly oozes, but it's worth it. There's nothing better than coffee with a warm sweet roll. I've lived on them for years." She leaned back in the chair. "You claim you want truth and justice for Cathy. That makes you the first—besides me. I told everything to a gal from the *Times*. She seemed interested, struck me as smart, and promised truth would be told. She lied. Lying and liars is all I run into these days. Convince me you're different. Cause I'll do whatever it takes to get the truth out."

"I met that *Times* reporter—Charlene."

"That's her name."

"Her paper wouldn't publish the story you gave her."

"I wonder how hard she tried to get it published. Demanding truth takes guts."

"She did give me your name."

Mary refilled her cup. "Yeah, she wiped her hands and gave it to you. She doesn't care—that's the beginning and end of it."

"She's got a lot of company."

Sean grabbed another roll. "These are great."

"I don't know where those bastards get these rolls. They never returned my phone, and I've been a prisoner here ever since the murder."

"You told the truth—that makes you dangerous. Now they're trying to figure out what to do with you."

Mary rose and stretched her thin arms above her head. "They're scared of a skinny old bag-of-bones like me. What a world."

She reached for the tray. "Want any more?"

"I'm good."

She set the tray on the kitchen counter. "I turned seventy-three last Tuesday and spent the day alone watching television and drinking coffee. I invited those bums out there to come in and share a cup on my birthday—maybe watch an old movie. They laughed."

She leaned on the counter, brushed back her thinning gray hair, and stared across the small room. "I can't remember the last time I was at a backyard barbeque drinking beer and eating potato salad." She wiped away a tear. "Time and life get away from us."

Sean grabbed his empty cup and set it on the counter. "We better hurry."

"I'm ready!"

Sean flipped on his video recorder while Mary dropped back in the easy chair.

"What happened that day—from the beginning?" Sean asked.

Mary gazed upward and smiled. "First, we're going to talk about Cathy—such a sweet and caring young lady. She took me grocery shopping and drove me to doctor appointments. She even checked in on me every morning before she went to work. She came from a small town in West Virginia—had a neat accent." Mary pointed to a picture on the wall of her and Cathy. "Wasn't she beautiful?"

Sean nodded. "Absolutely."

"She wanted to be an interior decorator. She'd watch a TV show where they'd go in and decorate a rich person's fancy apartment or big home, and then come over and tell me all about it over coffee. We drank a lot of coffee together."

Mary folded her skinny wrinkled hands. "Everything was fine until she went to work at the mayor's office answering the phone, running errands, things like that. Cathy had just turned twenty when Joe Delancey murdered her. That's when they stop calling you by your name and start using terms like corpse, body, or cadaver." She raised her voice. "Notice when a bigshot dies, they're still referred to as Mr. or Ms. Bigshot even though they're just as dead."

She leaned forward. "They figured Cathy as just another nobody. So, they frame a kid for her murder and close the door. And that's the end of it."

"Are you saying Mayor Delancey's son, Joe, was involved in Cathy's murder?"

"He did it—I saw it."

"Why'd he kill her?"

"Cause she wouldn't go out with him, and he's a jealous asshole. That's all there's to it."

"Take me through it so I can get it down as evidence."

"He'd been harassing her at work. She complained—they did nothing. He came by a couple of times and banged on her apartment door. The son-of-a-bitch even beat on my door once, screaming her name. I called the cops, but he'd gone. I'm not sure they'd have done anything anyway."

Mary walked over and straightened a picture on the wall. "She'd quit her job at the mayor's office Friday morning and got back home around noon. She came over and we went for a walk. I told her to move in with me till she got another job."

"What about her friends and coworkers?"

"Shit—what about them? Yeah, she reached out. And they turned their backs. They didn't want her troubles to become their troubles. Cathy told me she heard he beat up another girl in the office and nobody did anything. Cathy Mason would be alive if enough people cared. What do you think of that?"

"Not much."

"I don't know if getting the truth out will make a damn bit of difference."

"Truth always matters—let's see what it's worth these days. For Cathy's sake, and to find out what kind of world people prefer to live in."

"You're right. Anyway, that Friday evening Cathy bunked at my place. Around seven the next morning, she packed a couple of suitcases and threw them in the trunk of her old Plymouth. She'd decided to run to a small town she'd visited as a child somewhere in the Missouri Ozarks. She emptied out her bank account, and I gave her another five hundred. Going cash for a while would make it more difficult for that jerk to track where she went."

"Where'd she bank?"

"First Union has a branch about a mile from here. Why's that important?"

"Maybe she mentioned something to the teller about Little Joe. It might be worth looking into. You never know."

Mary shrugged. "My guess is the mayor's people have closed any loophole there. But like you said—you never know."

"What happened next?"

"We'd said our goodbyes. Around one-thirty, I heard these terrible screams from the courtyard. I pulled back the curtains and see Cathy lying on the ground and Little Joe kicking and stomping on her head. I opened the door and yelled while dialing 911. He's so focused on beating Cathy he don't even pay attention to me."

"Did you see anyone else around?"

"Folks must have heard the screaming, but no one tried to put a stop to it. And don't waste time asking people around here. They ain't going to get involved."

"How long did it take the cops to show up?"

"Two patrolmen got there in five minutes, an ambulance a minute later. Cathy's beautiful face—all covered with blood and bruises. The ambulance guys didn't work on her or try to revive her. They just threw her on a stretcher and drove off. I think they knew she was dead."

"Where did Little Joe run?"

"He was right there, blood on his shirt, pants, and shoes, telling me to keep my fucking mouth shut. The cops heard all that, and just stood there. Hell of a world—ain't it."

Sean nodded. "Nothing truth can't fix."

"I'll do my part."

"What happened then?"

"Those two cops weren't going to do anything, so I ran back inside my apartment and watched from the window. The mayor arrived with a gang of well-dressed goons, and later his chief-of-staff showed up. The patrolmen left while Little Joe, no cuffs—no nothing—stood there gabbing with his dad. I ran back out when Little Joe started to walk away."

Sean peeked through the blinds. "Go ahead."

"What are they doing?"

"They're laughing and fooling with their smartphones."

"They bragged about their degrees from big universities. They're just a couple of idiots."

Sean nodded and smiled. "Looks like we'll be given the time we need."

"Given how—by whom?"

"I'll tell you about it later."

When Sean got back to the couch, he said, "What'd you do next?"

"I got right in the face of the mayor and told him I seen it all. You know what he said?"

"Nothing would surprise me."

"He grabbed my arm and laughed.'"

"Is that where you guys left it?"

"I'd captured the whole thing on my phone—Little Joe kicking and beating on Cathy. I waved the phone at him."

"Liars have trouble with that kind of evidence. Their best chance is to make sure it doesn't get out. The powerful intimidate people, while mainstream and social media are pretty good at closing things down—even if brave folks post them. I haven't seen your video out there."

"They took my phone and laptop. Since then, I've been under house arrest, wondering what they're planning next. I know I'm a loose end."

"I've got your statement, but we need to corroborate your testimony. I wish I had your cellphone and the recording you'd made of the assault. But they either destroyed it; or tucked it away."

She unbuttoned her blouse, reached inside her bra, and handed Sean a small flash drive. "I copied it to this before they grabbed my devices. It should have everything on there. There's your proof. They searched the apartment and my purse, but not me. Maybe they figured I didn't think fast enough to do this. I just needed a way to share it."

He shoved the flash drive in his shirt pocket. "You do now." He looked out the blinds again. "It's time for us to leave. I can't leave you here—you're in too much danger."

"Where would I go?"

"My place, you'll be safe there. I'll study what's on this flash drive and figure the best way to share this evidence. We'll leave a few lights and the TV on. Is there a back way out?"

She pointed. "It's just a few feet drop from the kitchen window. They ain't watching because they think an old lady like me can't get out that way."

Sean dragged a chair next to the window, pushed out the screen, and climbed through while Mary tossed some clothes in an overnight case, along with a framed photo of her and Cathy.

"Hand me your suitcase and step up on the chair. I'll lift you out."

Mary tossed him the suitcase, and said, "Wait a minute." She ran over and placed the last four sweet rolls in a small plastic zipper bag. "No sense wasting these."

As they hurried to Sean's car, Mary pointed. "What happened to your pants leg?"

"I ripped it climbing out the window."

"Get me the right color thread and I'll sew it up good as new."

Thirty minutes later, Sean pulled in his underground parking space, and then he and Mary headed to the elevator. His three-thousand square foot condo was on the fourth floor.

While riding up the elevator, Sean said, "Thanks for choosing to step up—despite the danger."

Mary shrugged. "What choice? Telling the truth or letting them spread lies."

Inside the condo, Sean led Mary to one of the spare bedrooms. He hid the flash drive and recording he'd just made of her testimony behind some books in his study, and then went to the kitchen to put on some coffee.

A few minutes later, Sean handed Mary a cup. "Let's head to the balcony."

"Don't forget the rolls."

They passed the floor-to-ceiling brick fireplace and wall of books out to a large wooden deck overlooking coffee shops, jewelers, bankers, caviar, and privilege.

Mary leaned against the rail and glanced up and down the street. "Where's the thrift store?"

"That's on the other side of town near the homeless camp."

"There's the rub—how much is too much and how much is not enough. Truth provides direction on sweet rolls, justice, and everything else." She scooped up some jelly that had spilled on the plate. "Back at the apartment, you said you've made a commitment to yourself—and others. Who are these others?"

"I needed to see you, and I believe they helped make it happen. They're spirits from the other side. You can believe it or not, but here we are."

Mary gazed at the late afternoon sky. "I've always felt something bigger is out there. I'm glad spirits are on our side. It means we're doing right."

"I've reached out to them a couple of times, but they're not going to do this for us. That is—secure truth and justice. The task belongs to us—and the world."

"I'm up for it."

"And you're not alone—I've got a team working on this. We meet Fridays at the Green Tavern."

"I know the place."

"I'll introduce you at the next meeting, meanwhile make yourself comfortable. I'll study the video/audio evidence we got, and figure what to do next. I've got a guy digging into the mayor's financial situation. I'm hoping to create as many cracks as possible in his armor. Folks are less likely to cover for someone that's starting to look weak."

She took a drink, and said, "Do you live here alone?"

"Yep—all by myself."

"Ever married?"

"Almost—about five-years ago."

"You're young, you got time."

"We'll see."

She glanced over as she picked up a roll. "When you're not working, what do you do with your time?"

"I love to play chess."

"Me too! Are you any good?"

Sean grinned. "A lot of people think so."

"We'll play a game before this is over."

"Count on it."

After they finished their coffee, Mary glanced back inside the apartment. "I noticed all those books. Got anything from the Romantics?"

"How about works from Byron, Shelley, and Keats?"

"I'll start with Keats."

"Of course."

Monday evening, after beating on her apartment door for five minutes, the security people broke in and discovered Mary gone. Twenty minutes later, Dave Franklin, the mayor's chief of staff, arrived.

Franklin was in his mid-fifties, short gray hair, and stocky. He'd been running the mayor's machine for ten years. Before that he'd been based in London. His background was a mystery prior to that—even to the mayor. He had a short temper and always got things done.

At the apartment door, Franklin grabbed a security man by his shirt collar. "How the fuck did this happen? All you had to do was keep track of one old lady. Did someone bribe you guys to look the other way?"

The thin, twenty-something man, looked at his partner. "We're loyal—we don't know how this happened."

Franklin pointed. "She went out that window. She must have got help from someone." He faced the security people. "Are you sure no one got past you?"

They glanced at each other, and then one said, "No, sir. Nobody got by us—we would have stopped them."

"Pound on every door in this complex and find out if anyone seen anything. Tell them there's a ten-thousand-dollar reward for any information about her whereabouts." He tossed a vase against the wall as he left the apartment.

Franklin called the police chief. "She might be on foot, flood this area with patrol cars. Have them question every old lady they come across, and haul in anyone that seems suspicious. It's critical we find her."

"Will do—Mr. Franklin."

Franklin walked over to his car, waved off everyone, and called his contact in Zurich.

"Sir, that woman we were concerned about has disappeared."

"What's being done?"

"I've got everyone available looking for her. I've offered a ten-thousand-dollar reward for information on her whereabouts."

"Make it one-hundred-thousand dollars. And call the minute you got something. Our people don't like noise—even a little. We might have to terminate her."

"Yes, sir."

On the ride home, Franklin called a man named Tuck. "Grab the two clowns we had watching that old lady. Find out what they know about her disappearance. Call when you're through with them."

Tuesday morning, Sean was at his desk checking the material from the flash drive while Mary curled up on the couch reading.

He looked over. "This is brutal."

She shook her head. "Turn down the volume; I can't handle that horror a second time."

Sean's phone rang—it was Andy.

"My friend Jacob learned from an old cop buddy that city hall is going crazy. That Mary Pence gal is missing, and they want her bad. They've thrown a hundred-thousand-dollar reward out for her," Andy said.

Sean drew Mary's attention, and then said to Andy, "Do they have any clues where she might have gone or who might have helped her?"

"They don't know shit. They're watching the airport and bus stations—stopping people on the street."

"They know the trouble she might cause," Sean said.

"Have Janet or Phil heard anything?" Andy asked.

"I'll call Phil and see if it affects his and Janet's plans. By the way, where are you?"

"Me and Kevin are still at the camp."

"Slip Jacob a fifty—I'll cover it when we meet Friday."

"He's not doing this for money, but he could use it. Thanks!"

Sean hung up and turned to Mary. "You're public enemy Number One. They're looking all over town for you."

She set the book down. "I've arrived. It feels good—making them sweat a little."

Around twelve-thirty, Mary called out, "What about lunch?"

Sean grabbed his phone. "I'll have the deli send sandwiches, sides, and two large root beers."

"Anything will be fine. How much do they want for a sandwich in this neighborhood?"

"Depending on what's included ten dollars and up."

"I could buy a dozen smothered in mayonnaise baloney sandwiches for that kind of money."

He laughed. "Careful, people die from too much mayonnaise."

Tuesday evening, Phil and Janet were driving across town for dinner at the White Fox, a trendy restaurant frequented by the moneyed class and senior-level people from the mayor's office. Phil had made a reservation for seven o'clock.

At a stoplight, Phil glanced at Janet. "I hate driving there in this old beat-up car."

"Maybe you can get a rental next time. Sean would understand," she responded.

"Last week the valet laughed when I handed him the keys. What I need is a new car. It doesn't have to be a Mercedes, but something nice."

The White Fox, renovated from an old two-story brick building that once housed a bookstore, seated one hundred on the ground floor. A separate bar area had room for thirty. Its outdoor café, surrounded by a four-foot cast-iron fence, could accommodate sixty. That area included a large gas-operated stone fireplace where folks partied during fall and winter months.

Upstairs retained much of that old bookstore feel with its rugged hardwood floor and wall of bookshelves. Chrome-plated chandeliers hung from the vaulted ceiling.

Politicians, business, and cultural leaders often gathered in a private room on the second floor. A gold neon White Fox flashed above ten-foot oak entrance doors.

Dressed in black tuxedo with white tie, the doorman smiled as Phil slipped him a twenty.

They were a little early, so they headed to the bar until called. They entered through a pair of saloon-like doors and grabbed two stools at the end of the bar. A young attractive brunette named Jasmine took Phil's order.

After the drinks arrived, Phil turned to Janet. "You don't guzzle beer or chomp on pretzels in a classy place like this."

Janet surveyed the room. "It's so clean, and no cracked plaster or stains. The way a place should be when you're out on the town. I'll bet they ain't got any wobbly chairs."

Phil noticed a man with his head resting on the bar. "Even the drunks are better dressed and got more class. They don't flop on the floor or stand at the entrance begging for money like they do at the Green Tavern."

While Janet was in the ladies' room, Phil spotted a late edition of the *Times* left on the bar. Splattered across the front page in large font it read Mary Pence—$100,000 Reward. A recent photo of Mary along with a brief article accompanied the headline.

When Janet returned, Phil handed her the paper. "The kid they arrested for the murder of Cathy Mason now claims he got hired by this Mary Pence to do the job. They have other witnesses saying Mary and the victim were feuding. Maybe Sean and his so-called spirit friends got it wrong."

Janet grabbed the paper. "I could use a hundred-thousand bucks."

"First thing I'd get is a new car."

Flanked by three other men, a husky well-dressed man entered and took a seat at the bar. Phil overheard one of the people address him as Mr. Franklin.

Phil whispered, "That big guy posted the reward. The article says to get in touch with him if you got information."

"He's one of the people we're supposed to be spying on. He acts like the boss man over there."

"Sean mentioned that Mary gal the last time the team met. I wonder if he's found her."

"It's worth a hundred-thousand dollars."

Phil slid off the stool. "They just called us. Let's eat and think about this."

On the ride home, Janet turned to Phil. "Coming back from the ladies' room a guy stopped me and asked if I was with anyone. I said yes, but he still wanted my phone number. Can you imagine him pulling up to my address in his expensive car seeing water heaters and old washing machines lying about—and the smell of a dead dog? He wouldn't get out. Last winter a squirrel or rat got trapped and died inside my bedroom wall. I lived with that rotting stink for months."

She rolled down the window. "The bathroom at the White Fox is cleaner and smells better than anything in this part of town. I'm sick of the foul odor, broken glass, loud talk from those punk-ass kids, and gunshots. Everything's dead or dying around here."

She shrugged. "When I was young folks said I'd be going places because of my looks."

Phil flicked his cigarette butt out the window. "I used to think I had a future."

When they reached Janet's place, Phil walked her to the metal door, and said, "There might be something we can do about all this—who knows. I'll make reservations for Thursday night at the White Fox. Maybe we'll run into your new boyfriend."

Early Thursday, Sean received an electronic file from his old college buddy Fred Buckley at the brokerage house. The file included a spreadsheet outlining financial deals between Mayor Delancey and various oligarchs, crime lords, and foreign governments. The material wasn't sourced, but Fred indicated this would be supplied after they had a chance to talk.

Sean studied the material at his desk in the study while Mary relaxed on the couch. "This financial information from my buddy is explosive, we just need to source this data—or everybody will just deny it."

Mary looked over. "Don't expect the media to cover it—even if it's sourced. They're as corrupt as the mayor and his cronies—all part of the same gang. The radio and TV stations are running stories I was involved in Cathy's murder. This guy Franklin hands them a script and they run with it. Give him credit—he's an effective son-of-a bitch. But how are we going to get the truth out when all the information outlets are controlled by people who don't give a shit about truth?"

"I think we've got enough to prove who did the murder, and who helped cover it up." Sean pointed to the spreadsheet on his computer screen. "This financial data might scare some of the mayor's allies into running for cover."

"We're back to the problem of getting it out there. Mainstream media won't touch truth. Social media will pull down any posts that don't support their bullshit narrative, and then block you."

Sean's phone rang—it was Fred.

Sean picked up, and said, "Got the material you sent—great stuff. We just need to source it and we're done."

"I need something from you first," Fred responded.

"Sure—anything."

"My research stirred up a hornet's nest. Someone contacted my boss, and I got to meet with him to explain what I'm doing. You said 'superheavyweights' backed you in this play. I gotta have their names. That will provide the leverage I need to cover me. My boss understands shit like that—even if they're shadowy. If they're big enough, it might lead to a promotion a couple floors up."

Sean walked out to the deck. "I should have told you up front."

"That's OK. The material I sent shows nothing's left to chance these days. All we're doing is helping one gang of elite push out another gang. It doesn't matter to me whose coattails pull me upstairs. We can meet later at Harvey's Bar and break open a bottle. Who are they so we can wrap this call up?"

Sean gazed at a long lazy blue cloud. "They're spirits—and they're real."

"Is that some kind of code? Where are they located? Where do they bank? How did you meet them?"

"They're more powerful than anything in this world."

"Sure, sure."

"You got to trust me. I died a few weeks ago and met these spirits on the other side. They asked me to come back to seek truth and help right a wrong. Your research is part of that. I've got others working on this. I'll figure a way to make what I've gathered available to the public. I know that seems like long odds these days, but you'll be working to secure real truth and justice—maybe the first time in years. And that counts on the other side." Sean continued until he realized Fred had hung up.

Friday morning, Kevin and Andy hiked over to the homeless camp to get an update from Jacob. They stopped at a donut shop run by an old German couple named Hoffmann, and picked up a dozen chocolate donuts, plastic cups, and a two-liter container of coffee.

An ambulance pulled away as they arrived at the camp. They learned it contained the body of a middle-aged woman everyone called Sunny. She'd been at the camp for a couple of years and claimed to have been a grade-school teacher in Iowa. And that's about all anyone knew.

They spotted Jacob sitting on his favorite bench with a cigarette.

Andy held up the bag of donuts as they approached.

Jacob shouted, "Got anything in there for me?"

Andy handed him a donut and cup of coffee. "I see we lost Sunny. "

Jacob pointed. "I found her cold and stiff in her flower garden, head resting on that bed of purple Iris she loved so much. The ambulance people figured she'd been dead since sometime last night. Nobody heard anything, and I didn't see any marks of violence. A couple weeks ago she mentioned a pain in her lower back. Who knows—maybe she got weary of life and gave up. It happens a lot around here."

"Wasn't she from Iowa?"

"I think Des Moines."

"I don't remember anyone visiting her."

"Like most of us—she'll fade into the fog like she never happened."

Andy glanced at Kevin. "We'll add her to our prayer list."

"What about her garden? Those bright purple and orange flowers and sweet smells added a touch of elegance to this place," Kevin said.

Jacob leaned back on the bench. "I'm going to reach out to those kids from the local college. They drift over here a couple times a week. Maybe a couple of them would work the garden. That'll keep her memory alive—at least till the end of summer."

Andy nodded. "I think Sunny would like that."

A warm breeze scattered a small pile of nearby leaves while across the street folks from the camp drifted downtown to panhandle from their favorite corners. A few carried cardboard signs and folding lawn chairs. The cops didn't say much unless they got aggressive. Depending on how many hours put in, a day's take could range from fifteen to twenty-five tax-free dollars—a little more on holidays.

"You guys see the paper?" Jacob asked.

"The papers, TV and radio stations are all running a bullshit story tying Mary Pence to the murder. A hundred thousand is going to bring out the rats," Andy said.

Jacob took a drag and grinned. "The biggest rats are the one's pulling all these strings. The others are just little rats trying to move up or protect what they got."

"It took a lot of rats to get us here," Andy said.

Jacob added, "Most of the time rats don't think they're rats, or that they could ever be rats. Then one day folks make a choice—and some become rats."

"Is there a king rat?" Kevin asked.

Jacob flicked his cigarette. "There's always a pecking order."

A couple of bluebirds landed a few feet away. Seconds later they took off—each lugging a long fat worm.

Andy watched as they sailed across the street landing on the branch of a big oak tree. "There's a simple life."

"I wish I could fly—even for a while. You know—get away from all this," Kevin said.

Jacob shook his head. "There's no getting away from it." He tossed a small rock in the air and watched it drop to the ground. "Gravity is real just like two plus two always equals four. Same rules for rocks, birds, and man no matter how much illusion you throw at it. When you fuck-up there's a bill waiting to be paid." He coughed as he gazed across the street at the rows of tents, lean-to's, bedrolls, and folks shuffling about. "You flash a big wad of bills over there and you might not wake up the next morning. Half the camp—maybe more—would sell out that Mary gal or anyone for a lot less than a hundred-thousand bucks. There are rats everywhere—this place ain't any different."

Jacob dusted off his shoes, and then looked at Andy. "Got any more coffee?"

"Here you go."

He took a drink, and said, "They're gonna kill her as soon as they get her in custody. No lawyers, no trials, just found hanging in her holdover cell. It's all set—just waiting for the victim to show up. Then it's another 'case closed' due to suicide. That's the word from my guy in the mayor's office."

"Are you sure?" Kevin asked.

"He said the suicide note is already written and signed. How's that for efficiency."

"Damn!"

"Never underestimate rats, a lot are good at what they do."

Andy shrugged. "What about her handwriting? People will know it isn't hers."

"My guy said they got copies of her handwriting when they raided her apartment and had specialists put pen to paper. You know—she's sorry for what she'd done, felt despondent, etc. All very neat like they'd done it a few times before. Besides, no one's going to question any of this."

"We are!" Kevin yelled.

"And that puts you, me, and everyone else in this project in danger. Those pictures of the murdered girl, Cathy, you guys posted last week have got their attention. Don't agree to meet anyone claiming they got information—it'll be a setup."

Jacob set his coffee down and lit a cigarette. "This Mary has stirred things up really good. She must be quite a gal. We gotta make sure those city-hall gangsters don't get hold of her."

Andy handed Jacob a flip phone. "Call as soon as you hear anything. You can recharge at the library."

Jacob pointed as a bus pulled up with the name Goodhue Center painted on the side. "The Goodhue ladies have arrived." Folks rushed from their tents and assembled around the bus.

Andy laughed. "Right on time with their 'I care' packages. I got a delicious chocolate cake once from Doris. Man, she's a great cook."

"Remember that real short lady that brought trays of creampuffs? I ain't seen her in a while. Do you remember her name?" Kevin asked.

Jacob nodded. "Madelyn Jameson—her son came by and told me she fell and broke her hip and died in a nursing home. Twenty years from now her grandkids will be dropping off shit here." He took a drag, and said, "I won't be around—thank God."

Jacob spotted a couple of guys pushing their way to the front of the line. "I better straighten out those fucking knuckleheads."

"We ought to get going," Andy said.

Kevin shoved fifty dollars in Jacob's shirt pocket and reminded him to be careful.

On the walk home, Andy turned to Kevin. "I love listening to Jacob. He sure knows life."

Kevin laughed. "And about rats."

Andy pulled out his cellphone. "I'd better call Sean about that suicide stuff."

"Good idea."

Friday evening, a little past five o'clock, Sean and Mary parked near the front entrance of the Green Tavern.

Sean opened the passenger side door. "We're probably the first ones here."

Mary tapped a beer can out of the way with her right foot as she got out of the car. A half block down the street, a young man in tattered jeans and black cowboy hat sat stretched out drinking from a large brown bottle in front of a long-closed family hardware business.

She stared at the young man. "There used to be a penny bubble-gum machine right where he's at. I'd make my dad buy me a gumball whenever we went in there. The owner was a disabled World War Two veteran—nice guy. I used to hang with his daughter. My folks lived the next block over. We moved when I turned fifteen."

As Sean held open the tavern door, Mary glanced down the street. "He's baking in this heat."

A couple of old-timers sat at the bar arguing as Sean and Mary walked to the back and pulled together a couple of tables by the window.

Sean waved two fingers at the bartender. "How about a beer while we wait for the others?"

"You bet—nothing better than a cold beer on a hot day."

After Sean got back with the beer, Mary took a drink, and said, "This was the first place in the neighborhood to have air conditioning. To get out of the heat, us kids came in and bought root beer and lemonade." She pointed. "The owner would sit us over there so we wouldn't mix with the older customers. We had a small oscillating fan at home—that's it. Air conditioners are nice, but people used to get along without it. I still can."

Three blocks away, Kevin had just set down a container of fresh water and two plates of soft cat food.

As Molly and Gertrude rushed at the food, Andy said, "Slow down, girls, don't eat too fast."

Kevin checked the time. "We better head out."

"Let's go."

A block from their home, they noticed a thin gray cat following them.

Andy gazed over his shoulder. "Say hello to Henry."

"Henry?" Kevin asked.

"Yeah, I've named him after my uncle. He's been running around the neighborhood and I've fed him a couple of times. I think he wants to join the family."

"Let's check with Gertrude and Molly."

"He'll follow us home. We'll invite him in and see what they say."

Dressed in matching dark-blue shirts and tan trousers, they pushed open the tavern's faded green wooden doors.

Sean rose and waved them over. "Gentleman, this is Mary Pence."

Kevin shook Mary's hand. "You're a popular lady."

"Yeah, seems like lots of folks want to get hold of me. I never figured I'd be worth a hundred-thousand bucks."

Sean noticed a monogram across the back of the shirts in large red letters TIGERS. "Are you guys suggesting we name our team the tigers?"

Kevin laughed. "A bowling team donated their old uniforms to the thrift store. We got these shirts for fifty cents apiece, and the pants for a buck. Not a bad deal."

Mary grabbed a pretzel. "Careful, folks might think you're part of a gang."

They talked a few minutes, with Mary sharing growing-up stories from this neighborhood.

When the glasses ran low, Andy signaled Sean. "Let's get another round."

While the bartender refilled the glasses, Andy whispered to Sean, "Did you tell Mary about the suicide plans they have for her?"

"Yep—she's got a right to know anything we know. She's a tough old bird—she won't fold."

Sean looked at his watch. "Where's the rest of this team?"

They were well into their second round of drinks when Phil and Janet entered around six-twenty.

Andy raised his glass. "There they are—and those ain't thrift store outfits."

Phil wore a black blazer and tight gray slacks and sported a neatly trimmed mustache. Janet wore a light-blue cocktail dress with plunging neckline.

Janet glanced at Sean. "I'm thinking of joining a gym not far from the mayor's office. I do need to drop a few pounds. Plus, they say you hear all kinds of interesting stuff there."

Sean ignored her as he drew everyone's attention to Mary. "This brave lady wants what we want—the truth. We now have evidence proving who murdered Cathy Mason, and how the crime got covered up." He stood and gripped the back of his rickety wooden chair. "Our challenge is getting the information before the public, and hope enough people care about truth."

Phil pointed at Mary. "The media says she was involved in the murder. TV stations are interviewing people living at the apartment complex who said she had a beef with Cathy and told people she wanted her dead."

"And the *Times* just ran a front-page story with sources claiming Mary has a long criminal history," Janet said.

Mary laughed. "At twelve they caught me stealing a comic book from the dime store. Did my apologies to the owners and got grounded for a month. I've been clean since then—I swear."

Sean raised his voice. "Mary backs up what she's saying with evidence—which I've got."

"You better hurry—Mary's life is at risk," Andy said.

"How so?" Janet asked.

Andy looked at Mary, and then at Sean. "The mayor's gangsters plan on murdering Mary and making it look like suicide. Her suicide note is already written and signed. They just need to toss her into a cell and discover the body the next morning."

Phil leaned across the table. "How the hell do you know that?"

"My source has good connections at the mayor's office and police department. They've seen the note."

"Have you seen this supposed note?"

"No, but I trust my sources."

"That ain't evidence, that's not proof. It's just some guy saying something."

"It makes sense—them getting rid of Mary. Besides the perpetrator, she's the only eyewitness to the crime. And killing ain't any big deal to them," Sean said.

Phil pointed at Mary. "The media, the mayor's people, the justice department—they all claim this woman had been involved with the killing."

"Ain't you been paying attention—the system is fucked. No matter where you look it's politicized and corrupt," Kevin said.

"If that's true, then what's the point of any of this? If the system isn't capable of handling truth, what are we going to do with this so-called evidence?" Phil replied.

Janet waved her hand. "Maybe the spirits can provide us guidance."

Phil glared at Sean. "Yeah, we ain't heard from them in a while—if ever. Why don't you conjure them up and make them tell us what our next step should be? Since they got this whole thing started—it's the least they owe us."

A loud thud drew their attention to the other side of the room, where old Pete had fallen off his bar stool. The bartender and another patron dragged him to a table.

Sean ran his hands through his short red hair. "I'm back to see if people care enough about truth to get justice. The spirits want to know."

"Has this been a test?" Andy asked.

"You could call it that. But the score's not in. After we deliver truth's message, will enough people listen and demand real justice? A lot of folks are being tested."

"What if you don't pass?"

"You'll get those results on the other side."

Kevin elbowed Andy, and said, "I knew it from that first day we got called for a special mission. I felt those spirits tugging at me in this very room."

"I remember you saying so," Andy replied.

Phil shook his head as he glanced at Janet.

Sean rapped the table with his right hand. "We've got Mary's recorded testimony and actual video of the crime itself. It'll prove Little Joe murdered Cathy and it got covered up by the local power brokers and their allies in the media. I've also got information related to financial misconduct stretching from London, to Paris, to Moscow, and other places around the world. We've got enough to shake the rotten system and secure justice for Cathy—if people care."

"Mary's here, but where's the other evidence?" Phil asked.

"I'm getting ready to flood a number of sites and hundreds of friend's emails with the information and ask that it be shared with others. Once it gets rolling, I don't believe social and mainstream media giants will be able to stomp out the story."

"OK, so when do you plan on doing this?"

"I'm pushing the button Monday morning, that's the best time to explode news around the world. However; we can start the process tonight." Sean ran outside and opened the trunk of his car and returned with typed paper. He distributed stacks of fifty to each team member. "This is Mary's description of what she saw, dated and signed."

Sean glanced at Andy. "We hurried up and put this together after you called this afternoon about that suicide note stuff." He looked around the table. "Drop these sheets everywhere: libraries, supermarkets, even a church. Hand them to anyone you bump in to and tell them to pass it on. I'll also put this with the other information out over the Internet on Monday, but who knows between now and then."

After giving everyone their week's pay, Sean said, "It's time to find out if our world still wants truth and justice. Keep your heads down, and we'll meet in a couple of weeks. By then we'll have the answer."

Phil and Janet finished their drinks and hurried out.

Kevin watched the others leave. "They're sure in a rush." He and Andy shook hands with Mary, and then headed over to rouse barfly Pete and get him home.

Sean watched them hoist Pete on their shoulders and slow walk him out the door. "The world needs more folks like them and their friend Jacob."

"Who's Jacob?" Mary asked.

"He's a former security guard who's been a real help in all this. We learned about that suicide note from him. I never met him, but he seems like a stand-up guy."

"Some always show up."

"Let's hope that's enough."

After thirty minutes or so, Mary glanced at the door. "Let's go see that young man down the street. Maybe we can get him some help."

Sean rose out of his chair. "We gotta be careful. You're on their most-wanted list."

From the corner, they scoured both sides of the street and saw nothing.

Sean poked his head inside a few of the abandoned buildings, and then turned to Mary. "He's disappeared."

"He couldn't wander far—not in his shape."

They walked up and down the block until Mary stopped in front of a lot covered in weeds, clumps of dirt mixed with gravel, and empty beer and soda cans. "The dime store stood right here." She put her hands on her hips. "On Saturday mornings, I'd run in there as soon as Mom gave me my allowance—all twenty-five cents. After we got our buying done, we'd jump on our bikes and spend the rest of the day pedaling the neighborhood—feeling the breeze. Sometimes we'd end up at the park, somebody's house, or maybe the movie theater."

She smiled at Sean. "I never stayed mad or miserable for long—in those days."

Sean suggested they give up the search.

Kevin and Andy dropped off Pete and then headed over to the thrift store and bought a pair of tennis shoes—size eight, and then went to a drug store and picked up Band-Aids, rubbing alcohol, and a big bottle of aspirin—turning it all over to Pete's wife.

Phil and Janet drove around discussing what they should do.

At a stoplight, Phil turned off the radio. "Sean's wrapping this thing up which means no more paydays."

"What are we going to do?" Janet asked.

"Go back to being broke."

"You mean living on chump jobs and public assistance."

"It means no more trips to the White Fox or other nice places."

Janet slapped the dashboard. "No thanks!"

He hit the accelerator as the light flickered from red to green. "Look on the bright side. If Sean succeeds, we'll be able to celebrate bringing truth and something called justice into this crummy world. Our bonus comes when we meet up with those spirits on the other side."

"My bills are due now. I can't cover them with the promise of a tomorrow payday."

"Nobody can." He pulled into a fast-food lot and parked. "I'm sorry Cathy Mason got murdered, but that happens every day in this damn city. I never heard of her before all this. The media says this Mary was mixed up in the murder. Who are we to say she wasn't involved? That ain't our job."

"And we can't bring Cathy back."

"We've been working the wrong side of this track."

"You could be right."

"And why should we risk our necks to change the way things are? It won't make any difference in the long run."

"What about Sean?" Janet asked.

"He's never worried about money, or about his next meal, or keeping a roof over his head. That's the truth of it."

"What should we do?"

"Mary's worth a hundred-thousand dollars, and we know where she's at. For a start, let's cash her in to the authorities."

Janet hesitated, and then said, "They wouldn't harm her, and she'll get a fair trial. I'm sure that suicide business from Kevin and Andy is crap. But you said—for a start. What'd you mean?"

"We can make this pay long-term."

"How?"

"We'll approach Dave Franklin, the mayor's chief fix-it guy. He's managing the reward money. We'll meet him somewhere, maybe the White Fox, and make the deal for Mary. While we're talking to him, we'll get him to discuss incriminating or at least embarrassing things about the mayor, his son, or whatever. Using those slick recorders we got with Sean's money, we'll get it all on tape. After we get our money for Mary, we'll send him a copy of the recording and ask for a certain amount per month to stay silent. I haven't figured out how much, it'll depend on how juicy the recording is."

Janet's hands shook as she lit a cigarette. "Whew—shake a guy like that down! He's no fool. We could end up in the ringer just like Mary. Why not split the hundred thousand and run?"

"In a year that money's gone and we're back where we started. I thought you wanted to get away from all that broken glass, those creepy crawly things, and the bad smells."

"I do…I got to."

"Sure, there's risk, but those people won't sweat a few grand a month to us. Maybe we ask for a cozy job in the mayor's office instead. Trust me—it'll work."

She took a deep drag and tossed the cigarette out the window. "My life's never been good enough."

"This will fix it."

A bright-red convertible jammed with noisy teenagers honked as it rolled past Phil's car.

"You want to go in and get a hamburger and shake?" Phil asked.

"I need a drink…maybe a couple. Let's run over to Calico's, it's just a block from here."

Saturday morning, Andy brushed Henry's skinny frame while bawling out Molly and Gertrude for staying out all night. After breakfast of coffee and donuts, they planned to flood the surrounding neighborhoods with Mary's signed statement, ending up at the homeless camp.

Around eight-thirty, armed with fifty copies apiece, they headed to the thrift store where Kevin gave a copy to the old lady behind the counter, while Kevin distributed a half-dozen sheets to a group of men rolling dice in a nearby alley. They left copies at the laundromat, donut shop, and to a couple of guys hanging in front of a liquor store. They waved down cars and handed sheets to drivers. At Saint Margaret's, a soon-to-be closed Catholic church, Father Dolan promised to discuss and expand on Mary's message at Sunday services.

At a busy corner, Kevin shaded his eyes with his left forearm as he gazed at the cloudless sky. "Phil and Janet haven't contributed much—have they?"

"Nothing that I can tell," Andy responded.

"Last night they spent most of their time tearing down Mary. That's weird because the spirits told Sean that Little Joe did the murder. We learned that the first night—they were there. Maybe this reward money has blinded them."

"Sounds like it. And remember what Jacob said about rats."

"I wonder why Sean invited them in this."

"Who knows—maybe the spirits wanted them."

"I'll add them to our prayer list."

"Go ahead—we've had bigger challenges."

Kevin banged a rock off a metal stop sign as they passed a boarded-up gas station. A little past noon they arrived at the camp.

Sean carried a tray out to the deck. "It's a beautiful day. We'll have our coffee and lemon sweet rolls out here."

"Be there in a minute." Mary flipped a page, and then closed a book of Poe's short stories.

Sean poured the coffee, and said, "Poe is absorbing. I took a course on him in college."

Mary reached for a roll. "I sense melancholy there. His wife and mother both died young from consumption, he drank heavy, and knew poverty. Dead at forty, yet he left a great body of work for the world."

"Same rules apply to everybody—produce a well-lived life. It doesn't have to be a long life."

A nightingale landed on top of the deck railing, fluttered its brown wings and reddish tail, and then began to sing.

While Sean and Mary finished their sweet rolls, across town Phil contacted Dave Franklin.

Janet stared at the dim light showing through curtains on the second-floor warehouse office. "Last week they found a young girl mutilated not far from here. Why'd you pick this spot?"

A siren wailed in the distance as Phil lit a cigarette and leaned back in the car seat. "I mentioned the White Fox, but Franklin insisted on coming here—for privacy. He promised to bring the reward money. What could I do?"

Harper was a side street bordered by aging warehouses and light industrial businesses. The nearest retail lay five blocks away—residential even further.

Janet rolled up the car window. "I don't know. The parking lot's empty—like everybody's gotten the hell out of here. Who's going to be at this meeting?"

"Franklin said he'd bring a guy to safeguard the cash—no one else."

"Besides tossing him Mary, what did you promise?"

"I didn't give any names but said I could identify others who had been hiding Mary and spreading rumors about the mayor's son. That got him real excited."

"So we're ratting out Sean along with Kevin and Andy?"

"We don't owe them anything."

"I wouldn't like to see them get hurt—particularly Sean. He's been nice."

"You can stay in the car, and I'll make the deal—and keep the hundred thousand for myself."

"No—I'll go along. I don't like sitting alone in the dark."

"Did you bring your recorder?"

"It's in my purse."

"Turn it on." Phil emptied his cigarette pack and put his recorder inside. "Mine will be in my shirt pocket. He'll never notice it. It's almost nine o'clock. We'll leave the car here and walk over."

As Phil opened the door for Janet, he spotted three parked cars lined next to each other a half-block down the street, and in the other direction a couple of men standing at the corner next to the stop sign.

Janet grabbed Phil's arm as they crossed the street. "We've been here fifteen minutes and not a single car has driven by."

"Maybe this part of town shuts down after seven o'clock."

The chain-link gate had been pulled open and the guard station was empty as they entered the unlit empty parking lot. Phil wore a gray blazer, red tie, and dark-blue slacks while Janet had on a green pantsuit she bought that afternoon.

Phil squeezed Janet's hand. "Smile, we're making a big score and setting ourselves up to get a lot more. Maybe we'll have time to run over to the White Fox and celebrate tonight. Their bar is open till one in the morning."

Janet gripped the railing as they climbed the splintery wooden steps to the second-floor office. "How did Franklin sound on the phone?"

"Had a deep gravelly voice—sounded like someone used to getting his way. I shared just enough to show we could help, and then demanded he bring the hundred thousand in cash or no deal. He knew I was serious."

They heard voices from inside the office as Janet gazed at the dark empty lot. "I wonder how Franklin got here, or where he parked."

"Who cares—next week I'll be driving a new car and you'll be moving to Uptown."

Janet combed back her hair. "How do I look?"

"Like half of a hundred-thousand bucks."

The door swung open and a young man in jeans and a dirty blue work shirt signaled them in. He took their cellphones, promising they'd be returned after the meeting, and led them to a pair of wooden chairs. The tight little room held a small desk and a cloth-covered loveseat. The faint odor of engine oil rose from floor stains trekked in over the years from the loading docks.

Franklin, barrel-chested, in black trousers and white shirt with sleeves rolled up, faced them in a brown leather swivel seat with an angry looking grin. "Tell me where I can find Mary."

"What about our money?" Phil asked.

Franklin pointed to a suitcase on the desk, which the young man opened displaying bound stacks of hundred-dollar bills. "I'll let you know when it's yours. You said she was hiding out at a wealthy guy's condo."

"A guy named Sean has got her stashed and plans on releasing a video of her telling what she saw the day Cathy Mason got murdered."

Janet pulled a copy of Mary's signed statement from her purse. "This is what she claims she saw."

"We got that from her and this Sean guy," Phil said.

Franklin glanced over the document and threw it on the desk. "My people have seen these around town. It's just her claiming someone else did the murder. Any criminal can make up a story and sign it. That doesn't mean shit."

"But Sean said they got a video of the mayor's son doing the murder, and of the mayor showing up afterwards to start the cover-up," Phil said.

"Did this guy Sean show you that video?"

Phil looked at Janet. "We ain't seen it."

"Has he shown this video to anyone?"

"He hasn't, but he's gonna."

Franklin signaled and the young man got a bottle of scotch and three glasses from the desk drawer. After filling the glasses, the young man walked over and leaned against the door.

Franklin finished his drink and lit a cigar. "Let's start with this guy Sean, where he lives, and how he got connected to Mary Pence? What's his last name?"

"His name is Sean Kelly, a rich guy living at the Artemis Avenue apartments. That's where he's got Mary stashed."

"How does he know Mary Pence?"

Janet looked at Phil. "Didn't the spirits help him with that?"

"Nah, I think he got her name from someone at a newspaper in town."

Franklin raised his voice. "Who the hell are these spirits? What's their role in all of this? Who do they work for?"

"The guy claims spirits sent him back to seek justice in all this," Phil said.

"Sent him back from where?"

Janet reached into her purse to get a cigarette. "Back from the other side—after he died from drowning."

"Of course, we didn't believe him about that," Phil added.

"Do these spirits have names?"

"He never told us," Janet responded.

The young man at the door laughed as Franklin walked over and pushed back the curtains.

After refilling their glasses, Franklin sat and puffed on his cigar. "Did you think you could sucker me out of a hundred-thousand bucks that easy? Who are you two?" He looked at Phil. "We'll start with you."

"We're from the neighborhood, and we just want to help get this Mary off the streets. We met her yesterday at the Green Tavern with the others."

"What others?"

"Kevin and Andy have been helping Sean with all this. And they got a friend named Jacob who has contacts on the police force."

"Where can we find him?"

"He stays at the homeless camp. You know—the one on Arsenal Street."

Janet grabbed Phil's arm at the sound of footsteps and then voices outside the door.

Franklin put the bottle back inside the drawer, and then leaned forward on the desk. "We have a rich guy back from the dead, a broken-down bar, and a homeless camp. Oh yes, and spirits somewhere on the other side—beyond our reach. You got anything else?"

Phil nodded. "Sean referred to you as the mayor's fix-it guy. I think he's got stuff on you."

"What do you mean—stuff?"

"We could find out if we worked for you—as special inspectors or something."

Franklin grinned. "Hire you two!" He laughed as he walked around the desk. "Assuming anything you told me is true—you just ratted out all your associates. You're nothing but a couple of low-life hucksters trying to scam me out of a hundred-thousand bucks."

Janet dropped her purse and out popped her recorder on the floor.

Franklin scooped up the device. "Well, well, well—a recorder." He signaled for the young man to open the door. Three husky middle-aged men in jeans and gray sweatshirts rushed in and stood behind Phil and Janet.

As the young man closed the door, Phil stood. "We just came to make a deal and leave."

"Sit his ass down!" Franklin yelled.

Janet began to cry. "I didn't want to do this—he made me."

Franklin snapped the suitcase shut. "Dump their car—it's across the street. Toss his wallet and her purse on the desk and take them to that place on Bilzing Avenue. We'll find out how much truth they got in them."

Phil got tackled running toward the door, punched a couple of times, and dragged out, bleeding from the nose and lip. Janet lost one of her new shoes while being hurried across the parking lot and shoved into the backseat of a waiting car.

While Phil and Janet were being interrogated, Sean and Mary enjoyed a presentation of *Hamlet* at a small theater a few blocks from Sean's place. Mary had dyed her hair a dark brunette and wore thin-rimmed glasses. After the play ended, they stopped off at

Katz's Bakery and ordered coffee and a plate of glazed and jelly donuts.

Sean took a drink and picked up a donut. "This time next week we'll know where truth and justice fit in this world. I'm hoping it goes the right way—but you never know."

"What about the spirits?" Mary asked.

"It's up to us. Of course, they're always watching."

"I told you—I learned that as a little girl. There's a day of reckoning and you don't want to be stuck on the wrong side for eternity."

Sean smiled as the waitress refilled their cups.

Over the next hour they talked about the city, the richness of *Hamlet*, and their plans come Monday morning. After Sean finished off the last donut, he and Mary walked the two blocks to Eighth Avenue.

They were waiting for the light to turn when a neighbor from Sean's building came running over. "A group of men just knocked down your door, and then started pounding on other doors looking for you and some woman. I told them I didn't know shit, and they still searched my place. They were interrogating the doorman as I left."

He grabbed Sean by the arm. "Man, what'd you do?"

"I've threatened the world with truth. Even a little truth makes people nervous these days."

"They're more than nervous—they're mad. They flashed guns, pushed, and screamed at folks—even kids."

Sean thanked the man, waited till the guy disappeared down the street, and then turned to Mary. "We'll head back to Katz's for another cup and figure our next step."

Five minutes later, they were at their same window booth.

Their waitress walked over with a couple of menus. "You back for more donuts?"

"Just coffee this time," Sean said.

Mary glanced out the window as a taxi sped by. "Maybe they won't bother you and your friends if I just turn myself in."

"No chance. We're facing this together."

Sean tapped his phone a few times and then looked at Mary. "I've just sent it out." A minute later, the explosive material was on its way to hundreds of Internet sites and email addresses.

Mary shook her head. "What if facts don't matter—even on video?"

"We'll find out."

Sean's phone rang—it was Kevin.

"What's up?" Sean said.

"My friend Jacob just called and said a dozen men showed up at the camp searching for Mary—and him. He hid out over at the park and waited till they left."

"Yeah, they've also been to my place."

"I wonder how they've made all those connections."

"They're good at things like that—a lot of practice."

Andy grabbed the phone from Kevin. "We're staying away from the Green Tavern and the camp."

"Good idea. I just sent out the material, so hang close to home and stay off the phone. I'll call in four or five days."

Sean had just finished his third cup when his phone rang again—it was Janet.

"What's up?" Sean said.

"We gotta talk."

"Go ahead—talk."

"In person—we need to meet now. And make sure to bring Mary."

"Can't it wait?"

"No!"

"Is Phil with you?"

"Yes, but he can't come to the phone. Where are you?"

"I'm out roaming the neighborhood." He glanced at Mary. "Why does Mary have to be there?"

"I can't tell you anymore over the phone."

Sean signaled Mary they were leaving, and then said, "You know Katz Bakery?"

"We can find it."

"We're there now."

"Great, see you in a few minutes."

Sean tossed a twenty on the table and grabbed Mary's hand. "Let's get the hell out of here."

They dodged a delivery van as they raced across the busy street and ducked into a small alley just as three police vehicles and two black sedans pulled up and half dozen men rushed into the bakery.

People inside the bakery were forced to line up against one of the walls, while two uniformed officers stood at the entrance preventing anyone entering or leaving. A gray-haired woman about Mary's age and height was dragged out of the bakery in handcuffs and pushed screaming into one of the sedans, which then sped off.

Sean whispered as they crouched behind a small dumpster. "I hope they let her go after they figure it isn't you."

"What about Janet and Phil?"

"I'm not sure."

Mary smiled as they fast walked to the other end of the alley. "I feel good about what we've done—no matter what happens."

Sean winked. "Cathy knows and appreciates it."

A cab dropped them off at a small out-of-the way motel called Spiro's where they registered as Mr. and Mrs. Smith.

Sean and Mary spent the next few days eating pizza, spaghetti, and salads at a neighborhood restaurant while monitoring television, radio, social media sites, and Sean's emails. By Monday morning, the videos, particularly the one showing the mayor's son beating Cathy, had appeared on several social media sites. That afternoon, a small business channel had mentioned the financial piece of the story. Sean noticed some Internet chatter and personal sharing of the videos.

Midday Tuesday, while walking to the restaurant, Sean turned to Mary. "It's disappointing none of the mainstream networks have even mentioned the story. They must be aware of the videos by now."

Mary laughed. "When truth interferes with their narrative—they're stuck. They might ignore it, or claim its fake, or maybe fine-tune the narrative considering the new information. They're waiting to be told how to respond to this."

"You're pretty sharp."

"I've learned a few things in seventy-three years."

Franklin's cellphone rang—it was Zurich.

He ran and closed his office door. "Yes, sir."

"We're not satisfied with the direction of things."

"Yes, sir."

"We recommend a change—both the mayor and his son."

"I've been thinking along those same lines. We're spending too much time and effort cleaning up for those two."

"When can we expect to see that change?"

"It'll be finished within a week—maybe less. The deputy mayor is ready to step right in. She's reliable and won't saddle us with these kinds of issues."

"Our friends were upset at the release of the financial information. We've sealed the leak here and had a man at the receiving end named Fred-something fired from his position. Are there any loose threads before we close this up?"

"After we take care of the mayor and his son, I'll give the media a new story compatible with the video that got released."

"Is that it?"

"I've had to deal with a couple of third-rate grifters. Nobody's gonna miss them. In a month this will be forgotten."

"I'll tell our friends."

"Thank you, sir."

"My God—I didn't expect this," Sean said.

Mary looked up from the magazine. "What happened?"

"The *Times* reports the mayor and his son got killed in a car accident late yesterday."

She hurried over. "Where'd this happen?"

"Out on Highway 94, car went over a cliff after it failed to navigate a dangerous curve. The mayor was driving with his son in the front seat—no other passengers. It says they had been heading to a private meeting with political donors."

"That's weird."

"What is?"

Mary put her hand on Sean's shoulder. "The mayor's chauffeur drives him everywhere. Watch the news or see him on the front page—that fat bastard is always getting out of the back seat of a limo. Letting everyone know he's a bigshot. There's something odd about this."

"You don't think it was an accident?"

"Nothing would surprise me."

"At least the mayor and his son are facing real justice for what they did."

Sean smiled. "The article says they've decided to reopen the investigation into Cathy Mason's murder—in light of new information. We stirred that up."

"What do you think they'll do about me and the others who helped you? They might still figure us a threat."

"We'll hide here a few more days and see what they do."

Franklin moved quickly. Within hours of the mayor's death a replacement had been sworn in. A week later the local prosecutor released the young man held in Cathy Mason's murder and stated Mary Pence was no longer considered to be involved in the crime. The hundred-thousand-dollar bounty for her capture was withdrawn.

Ten days after being sworn in, the city's first woman mayor held a press conference on the steps of city hall—Franklin at her side. The assembled roared approval as she denounced the crimes and corruption of the previous administration and promised REFORM.

After hearing she was no longer being pursued, Mary flipped the TV off. "Well, that's that."

Sean leaned back on the sofa. "We cornered them with truth—and they weren't happy. Truth is like that. It can make folks uncomfortable, confused, and sometimes mad as hell. People and societies decide how much truth they want or tolerate—it's a choice. It doesn't always come easy—if it comes at all."

"It can sure get messy and complicated—even dangerous."

"Folks have been wrestling with truth since the beginning of time. Some people never get it, or don't want it. I've learned a lot this second-time around."

Mary nodded. "And Cathy's killer is being held accountable."

"That was always in the cards. We just sped things along."

"It sounds like these bums have given up on me—but what about you? They know where you live."

"I'm sure they don't want to stir this pot up again. Besides, I'll be returning to a place beyond their reach."

"Are the spirits making you return?"

"No, it's my choice. But my work is done here. Besides—there's a lot of folks I want to look up."

"Are you sure you'll find them up there?"

"That's a mystery we all get to solve."

"Make sure to put in a good word for me."

"I don't have to. He's always watching."

"It's been a wild few weeks, and you probably saved my life. Before you go back let's get a package of cherry sweet rolls and play that game of chess you owe me."

Sean hugged her and then opened the door. "Let's go."

The Ironton Exit

"I want you in the office, first thing Monday morning," Stan said.

"Why, what's the problem?" Greg responded.

"The auditors have questions about the financial reporting, and your name came up."

"There's nothing wrong with my entries."

"Just get your ass in here Monday." And then he hung up.

    Auditors bothered the hell out of Greg Anderson. They could make it look like you had done something wrong when you hadn't. He wondered if Monday, a week before Christmas, might be his last day with Achilles International. At fifty-four, graying hair, and the stigma of getting let go would make it tough to start over.
    Greg lit a cigarette, slipped on his tan parka, grabbed his laptop, and headed out the door early Sunday morning for the six-hour drive. He figured to check into a motel near the office and drive over Monday for the news.
    Four hours later the windshield wipers on Greg's Jeep were barely keeping pace with the hard driving snow. The highway was unplowed, visibility three car lengths, and speeds down to ten miles per hour. He'd been making great time until he ran into this mess. He wondered why this storm hadn't been predicted as he passed a silver sedan that had spun off into a ditch.
    When the radio announced a multi-car pileup a few miles ahead, Greg pulled off the next exit to the service road. From there

it was just three miles to Bascombe Avenue, a narrow two-lane blacktop leading to Ironton—his hometown. Rather than sit in slow or no-moving traffic, Greg decided to spend an hour or two sightseeing old hideouts and haunts he hadn't seen in years; by then the roads would be cleared and traffic back up to speed. The office was just two hours away—he figured he had plenty of time.

Greg hit the edge of town and spotted Bumpy's gas station. As he pulled in, he remembered as a twelve-year-old he bought cigarettes from the vending machine in there for fifty cents a pack.

While the tank filled, Greg leaned against his black Jeep and studied the worn white-brick building and its three empty service bays. A snow-covered tow truck that looked twenty years old sat idle. Other than a faded-green Chevy station wagon parked near the door, Greg's was the only vehicle there. After filling up the tank, he remembered that Bumpy's always kept a warm pot of coffee on.

Greg swung open the metal door, tapped the snow off his shoes, and spotted a young man in jeans and red-plaid shirt standing behind that old wooden counter. "Can I buy a cup of coffee?"

"Pour yourself one, it's free," he replied.

Greg filled a white plastic cup, and leaned against the counter. "It's been forty years since I've been here. I notice the sign still says Bumpy's. I guess he's long-retired."

"He dropped dead of a heart attack twenty years ago while replacing brakes on a car in that first bay. He was my grandfather."

"I ran in here as a kid and bought soda—even cigarettes. Bumpy was a good guy, and a World War II veteran like my dad. Hell, everybody's dad was a veteran in those days. At least he died doing what he liked."

"My dad still owns the place, but we just sell gas."

Greg took a drink while staring out the window at the snow-covered street and yards. "I remember your grandpa had this old floppy hound dog named Luther that used to lie on a brown rug next to the cigarette machine. Every time I'd come in he'd raise his head and bark like he was saying hello."

"My dad talked about that dog all the time. Luther was part of the family."

The young man poured himself a cup, and said, "Today was supposed to be clear. You can't count on anyone these days, even weathermen."

"Yep, there's lots of ways to get screwed. Just about anyone can do it to you."

"I guess I'll close around noon and head home. There's a football game I want to watch."

Greg thanked the young man for the coffee, and turned as he opened the door to leave. "If not for the snow, I wouldn't be here. Maybe it'll turn out to be a good thing."

"Yeah, who knows?"

The Jeep skidded as Greg swung onto snow-packed Bascombe Avenue. Three blocks later he made a right turn onto Harper Street. He passed homes he knew as a kid, and then parked in front of 315 Harper. The green shutters were gone, along with a piece of siding. A late model blue Mercury sat in the driveway.

Pelted by blowing snow, Greg walked to the back, gripped the chain-linked fence, and stared. That large oak tree he loved to climb was gone. He remembered playing kickball, tag, and hanging out with friends here. There was Mom, standing on that wooden porch in her green apron calling him in for supper, while Skippy barked and chased squirrels clutching acorns, or rabbits cutting through the yard.

A middle-aged woman, wrapped in a beige terry-cloth bathrobe stuck her head out the back door. "Who are you?"

Startled, Greg looked over, and said, "I played in this yard, and grew up in that house. I just came back to take a quick look."

As she closed the door, she said, "OK, but hurry up."

Greg left when he noticed her watching through the window. He drove the next block over to Tay Avenue and passed his first girlfriend Karen's home—a small ranch built after World War II. Like all the houses in the neighborhood, it used to be packed with lots of kids and often a grandparent or two. In those days, Karen was just a couple of backyards away. He still thought of her and wondered how she was getting along.

Greg drove to the end of Tay Avenue. Across the street was Saint Michael's Church and School, both founded in 1890. Those old brick buildings were a ten-minute walk for Greg and most kids in the neighborhood. It's where he got baptized, confirmed, and with friends spent his grade school years learning from the nuns how to read, write, and all about God.

Greg crossed Bascombe, parked near the school, and scanned the empty church lot. Where was everybody? It's Sunday! A peek in the first-grade window showed more emptiness: no desks, charts, clock on the wall, or crucifix above the door. Other rooms were in the same shape. He remembered gazing out those windows counting minutes till the bell rang for lunch or end of the school day. Those Fridays seemed to take forever to get to three o'clock.

He was leaning against the building thinking of the fun he had inside there, when he spotted fresh tire marks where the principal used to park. From there a single set of shoe tracks led to the church. Seconds later Greg opened a door he hadn't been through in forty years. The wooden pews were there, but not the vessels of holy water, the statue of Saint Michael, or the altar. In the dim light it felt like half the church had gone missing.

A voice called out. "Can I help you, young man?"

Greg spotted a woman sitting alone in the last pew. "Yes, ma'am. I hope you can."

Drawing closer he noticed her thick gray hair and wrinkled face and figured she had to be in her seventies—at least. A heavy black winter coat was slung over the pew in front of her, and she held what looked like a prayer book.

Greg stood at the end of her pew. "My family used to attend Mass at Saint Michael's. I graduated from the school—did all eight grades."

She signaled for him to come closer. "What's your name? I bet I know you and your folks."

Greg sat a few feet from her. "My name is Greg Anderson."

Without hesitating, she said, "And your dad's name is Ed, and your mom Dorothy."

"Goodness!"

She set her book down, and scooted closer to Greg. "I taught and was principal here for fifty years."

He thought a moment, and then said, "You're Sister Caroline."

She nodded. "It's been a long time. I love meeting former students. What brings you to this small corner of life?"

"The snow backed up the highway, so I detoured here for a few hours."

"Whatever it took—I'm glad."

Greg glanced around. "What happened?"

"They closed the school twelve years ago, then the church eight years ago. Not enough students, not enough parishioners, and now not enough clergy. I cry and pray about it all the time."

"Whatever happened to Father Hederman?" Greg asked.

"He passed away three years ago at the retirement center for priests. He was Saint Michael's pastor for forty-eight years. He was a good man—very humble."

"I liked him. He let you square things with God by reciting one Our Father and three Hail Marys. He was strict, but fair."

She leaned back in the pew. "I'm retired and staying at the Mother House. Saint Jerome's is still open, and we receive the Sacraments over there."

"I saw the tire tracks where someone dropped you off."

"The granddaughter of one of my old students drives me over for my Sunday visit. I'll call her when I'm ready to leave. Sometimes other retired sisters join me and we make a day of it. During the winter months we keep that old boiler going and run the temperature at sixty degrees. I do a lot of praying here. This will always be God's home—you know."

Greg nodded. "I've knelt and prayed in every one of these pews. In the early grades, you used to catch us trading holy cards during mass."

She laughed, and said, "I remember."

Greg looked where the altar used to be. "There were thousands of soul-searching sermons here. I wonder how much good they did?"

"God knows, and that's all that counts."

They talked a while, and then Greg noticed several bulging black plastic bags in the back of church.

He pointed. "What's that?"

"They're filled with ornaments and garland to decorate a tree near the pond. It catches people's attention driving past. It's been my own little project."

"I can help, if you're going to do it this morning."

She grabbed her coat. "Let's go."

Greg picked up the plastic bags, and they slow-walked to a patch of woods next to the church. The three acres contained long-needled pines, some birch trees, and several large oaks. The space also included a small pond with a couple of cast iron benches resting a few feet from its bank.

She led Greg to a six-foot tall Scotch pine. "This pine helps me keep Christmas at Saint Michael's."

Greg set the bags next to the tree.

"We'll start with the garland," she said.

"Yes, Sister."

Fifteen minutes later the tree was wrapped with bands of bright gold, brilliant reds, and shiny silver.

Sister handed Greg a box of hooks. "I'll give you an ornament and point where it goes."

"Yes, Sister."

After the last ornament, she pulled a large star from the bag. "This goes on top. Flick that little button, it lights up."

Greg secured the star to the top of the tree, and they watched it flash red, then gold, then back to red.

Arms folded, she stepped back and smiled. "This catches people's attention as they drive by. Not what it used to be around here, but it'll do."

"First tree I've helped decorate for Christmas in a long time. It felt good," Greg said.

He walked a short distance and pointed at the long steep hill that ran from the back of the church. "When the snow hit we'd grab our sleds and spend hours sailing down that hill. Maybe build a snowman later. There was me, Joe, George, and Jack—always the four of us. That was forever ago."

"I remember. I'd listen to the shouts and laughter from my office on the second floor. A couple of times I felt like grabbing a sled and racing somebody down that hill. I had so much fun watching you kids."

"A half hour after snow arrived there'd be twenty of us flying down that hill—or having a snowball fight. Now it's computer games and social media. Fun ain't what it used to be."

Sister brushed the snow off one of the benches. "What have you been doing with your life?"

Greg hesitated, and then said, "I'm divorced, and have a grown daughter I never hear from. I went to college, got a degree in accounting, and have worked for the same company the last twenty-three years. It's been a living, but not much of a life. After tomorrow, I'll know if it's made a turn for the worse."

"Trouble?"

"Ain't been yelled at like that since the fifth grade. Only difference is my boss used words most nuns wouldn't."

"The Sisters will be happy to pray for both of you."

"Thanks, Sister."

"Keep your faith and things will work out."

Greg watched the flashing star atop the tree. "Life used to be so good."

She nodded. "My first week at Saint Michael's seems like yesterday. Remember those Friday fish fries, bingo games, and school picnics?"

"You're making me wish I could've stayed twelve."

They talked, and then Greg said, "I drove past Karen Stuart's house on Tay Avenue. We went to Saint Michael's together—all eight grades. She was smart and nice. I liked her."

"She's still around. Her husband got killed in a car accident about five years ago. Her last name is now Brown. She lives a few blocks from our Motherhouse here in Ironton. I see her at Mass most Sundays over at St. Jerome's. She's such a sweet lady. I'm sure she'd love to hear from you."

Greg took a deep breath, and shrugged his shoulders.

The temperature had warmed, causing snowmelt from surrounding trees limbs to pelt the pond like rain. They watched a big white rabbit hop through the slush and disappear down a hole.

Greg pointed where he and friends had buried a turtle, and then flicked a pebble into the pond. "The fish in that little world get to live their whole lives here. You think they know how good they got it?"

She laughed, and said, "I'm seventy-five, and this has been my home for fifty years. I've been happy here, and so have you."

"I've got my graduating class picture, and can still name everybody," Greg said.

She gazed up as the sun burst through the clouds. "Last summer, Sister Margaret rescued a stray puppy right here at the pond, and then found its owners. How's that for small town news. We celebrated at the convent. It even made the local journal."

"Stories with happy endings are good news everywhere."

She shoved the empty plastic bags in her coat pocket. "You mentioned you're an accountant."

"I'm a good accountant."

"Even small towns need accountants. The Sisters could use bookkeeping help, and there are still enough businesses around to keep someone busy. Of course small towns don't pay like the big city."

"We never had much money—nobody around here did."

Sister waved as a car driving by honked. "That's Steve Carlson and his wife Joan. They both graduated from Saint Michael's. I've been to their home for dinner a number of times. Nice folks."

Greg checked his watch. "I should get going, the highway must be clear by now. Would you like a ride to the convent?"

"That's OK, there's a lady I'll call to pick me up. Besides, I need to stay and pray that you and your boss work things out." While they walked back, Sister mentioned the Christmas Mass schedule at St. Jerome's.

Greg held open the door of the old church, and said, "This visit came out of nowhere, and I'm glad it did."

She tapped him on the shoulder. "Wait while I get you something." She returned with a holy card featuring Saint Michael. "And don't trade it away."

"Yes, Sister."

Greg rolled down the car window as he left the church parking lot. The sun had shoved aside the overcast, and warmer air swept away most of the snow, leaving everything with a fresh, clean feel. He thought about Karen as he turned onto the highway.

Lost and Found in Glasgow

It was 1959 in a bustling subdivision called Glasgow Village, Missouri.

After they recited the Pledge of Allegiance, Miss Kinsky, a popular teacher in her forties, faced her class. "Welcome to the sixth grade. Before we open our math books, I want to briefly mention our class project."

She leaned forward at her desk. "Our semester project will investigate and highlight something or someone important to Glasgow Village. There've been great projects in the past and I expect this one will be just as rewarding. We're off next Monday for Labor Day, so next Tuesday I'll expect an idea from each of you."

Gary Vincent, a smart kid planning to be a writer, tapped his buddy Tom on the shoulder. "I'm gonna find our project this weekend."

Tom swung around. "It's all yours."

Saturday morning, Gary slid on a dark-green sweatshirt and grabbed his project notebook.

As the wooden screen door banged shut, his mom yelled, "Be back by lunch."

Gary checked out the busy shopping center down the street. Built in the early Fifties with the rest of the subdivision, it had a grocery and drug store, a dime store, along with a barber shop and hair salon. Gary jotted a few notes, bought a pack of baseball cards at the dime store, and headed to the ball diamonds at the bottom of Grampian Road.

Don't Pass the Exits

These fields hosted baseball and softball games then soccer in the fall. Gary remembered breaking his leg rounding third base and his embarrassment when his mom ran onto the field screaming. He waved at a couple of kids playing catch and headed home.

A block from his house, Gary sensed something behind him. He turned and spotted a small animal scurry behind a rusty gray sedan parked in the street.

Gary circled and then looked under the car. Nothing there but a patch of oil.

"You're late." Gary's mom shouted from the dining room.

Saturday lunch was always a bowl of chili for Gary and his dad, and a plate of hot tamales for his mom and sisters.

As Gary sat down, his mom said, "Where did you get off to?"

"I searched the neighborhood for school project ideas. I've got more looking to do this afternoon."

"You're done for today. You've got the lawn to cut this afternoon. Later we're heading to the drive-in to see that new Cary Grant spy movie."

His sister Pat laughed, and said, "Don't forget to rake and bag."

Gary slid his foot under the table and kicked her on the shin.

After Sunday services, Gary changed and hurried out the back door before his mom found something for him to do.

At the corner, Gary ran into his buddy Tom. "I'm hunting for project ideas. If Hemingway can get stories in Africa and Europe, I can find something in Glasgow."

Tom shrugged. "I'm heading to Jerry's for a card game."

"See you at school on Tuesday."

Gary passed a mud-covered field graded for more ranch-style houses. The contractor, a guy named Wilson, built all the homes in Glasgow Village. Gary thought he might make a good story and started to jot some notes when a small charcoal-gray dog poked its head from behind a backhoe.

Gary whistled, and said, "Come here, boy."

The little dog approached and sat a few feet away.

Gary brushed dirt from its back, and said, "It looks like you've been playing in mud." He patted the dog's thin frame. "You need to get home. Your owner must be worried."

The dog bounced to its feet, barked, and followed as Gary continued up the street.

After a few minutes, Gary glanced back. "OK—tag along."

Gary and the dog cut through woods as a soft breeze pushed leafy branches and bushes clinging to their last colorful shades of summer. Jumping over a log they spooked a rabbit hiding in the bushes. On the way to an old granite quarry they passed a box turtle munching a June bug.

The quarry, a man-made crater the length of a football field, sank sixty feet in places. Kids snuck in despite the *Closed Keep Out* signs and a chain-link fence. A gravel road led to the quarry which was surrounded on three sides by woods. A fast-moving creek ran along its north side.

While Gary stared at the played-out hole the little dog suddenly barked then tore through the underbrush running past a small poplar tree about a hundred feet away.

"Wait up," Gary shouted.

He circled a patch of poison ivy and spotted the dog next to a stone jutting out of the ground.

Gary approached. "What have we got here, boy?"

He grabbed a stick and scraped away dirt and weeds revealing the name Sarah Dunham with the dates 1810 to 1822 engraved on the stone. Another stone showed Jessica Dunham, 1790 to 1835. Over the next twenty minutes he'd uncovered other Dunhams and a Parker.

Gary faced the dog. "How'd you know about this?" After a few seconds, he said, "Not saying—huh? Well, the least I can do is get you something to eat."

He glanced at his companion. "I'm gonna call you Pepper."

Gary snuck in the kitchen and filled a bowl with water and scooped all the leftover pot roast onto a dish. Pepper licked the plate clean, drank a little, and settled next to Gary under the shady weeping willow tree in the middle of the back yard.

From the kitchen door, his mom yelled. "Where've you been?"

Before he answered, she walked out on the porch. "Whose dog is that?"

"This is Pepper."

"Are those my dishes?"

"He's all bones. I had to feed him."

"He's finished. Send him home."

"We can't just turn him loose—he'll starve or get run over. I don't know who owns him. He ain't got a collar."

"Then how do you know his name is Pepper?"

"I named him."

His mom leaned on the banister, stared for a few seconds, and then said, "Haul that plastic tub out of the garage and give him a bath. We'll take care of him till his owner shows up."

"Mom, you won't believe what Pepper helped me discover."

"Tell me after you've cleaned him up." She walked back in the house and shouted, "Honey, your son brought home another mouth to feed."

Gary rubbed Pepper's back. "You get to stay."

Pepper splashed in the soap suds while Gary removed burrs, clumps of dirt, and small leaves tangled in his short charcoal-colored hair.

From the porch, his sister Pat asked, "Where'd you get that skinny mutt?"

"None of your business."

"Mom says we all get to play with him."

"Don't forget—he's my dog."

Gary wrapped Pepper in a cotton bath towel and carried him to his bedroom. A minute later his mom stood at the door. "You said you discovered something."

"Pepper helped me find a bunch of graves near the old quarry. They date back over a hundred years."

"I told you not to go in that quarry!"

"It was in the woods next to the quarry. I counted five graves."

"Those woods are village property. I'm sure they don't want you disturbing graves."

"Pepper knew about it. The grave markers are half-buried under dirt and brush. I'll bet nobody knows about them."

She smiled at Pepper, and said, "He looks worn out. I wonder where he belongs."

After his mom left, Gary tossed the damp towel in the hamper then hugged his new companion. "We'll have a lot of fun together. My sisters are OK, but don't listen to them."

Pepper let out a ruffled bark then curled up next to Gary's pillow and fell asleep.

Tuesday before class, Tom asked, "What's new?"

Gary closed his locker. "I discovered a lost graveyard."

"Where?"

"Those woods near the quarry. I counted five graves—so far. They date back over a hundred years."

"I wonder who they were."

"I'm gonna ask Miss Kinsky to make finding that out our class project."

As they headed down the hall, Gary said, "Oh, yeah, I got a new dog."

"Dang—I'll stop by after school."

After the Pledge, Miss Kinsky said, "Now we'll decide on a class project."

Judy raised her hand. "I think we ought to do a story about my sister's softball team. They came in fourth in the state tournament last year."

Tom turned to Gary. "Oh brother."

Kathy Dalton said, "Why don't we write a letter to President Eisenhower and tell him what a great job he's doing. We can sign it and maybe he'll answer back. He might even call or stop by."

"That's why she's in the dumb row," Gary whispered to Tom.

Other suggestions included a class hula hoop contest, the value of a close-by pharmacy and grocery store, and a bio of Pastor Jefferson.

Miss Kinsky pointed. "Gary, let's hear from you."

"There's a graveyard near the quarry with born dates going back a hundred years. I think we should find out who those people were," Gary responded.

"How'd you discover this?"

"My dog Pepper led me there."

"How'd he know about it?"

"He hasn't told me."

She smiled, and said, "Of course that makes him part of this story. We'll have to find out who owns the property where the graves are."

"My mom said it belongs to the village."

"This idea has possibilities. Tell our custodian Bill where to find the graves. I'll ask him to drive over this morning and take a few photos. If it is an old graveyard, then I'll check with the mayor to see if it's on village or private property."

"It's way back in the woods. I'll have to go along to show him."

"All right, I'll get you permission to leave school grounds. "

"He's making the whole thing up," Judy shouted.

Miss Kinsky tapped her desk for quiet. "Let's hear a few more ideas, and then we'll get to our history books.

After school, Tom ran over to Gary's and watched a terrier-sized dog tear around the backyard barking at the neighbor's golden retriever.

Tom whistled, and said, "Whew he's got a lot of energy. Where'd he come from?"

Gary opened the gate. "I don't know, but there's something special about him."

"Like what?"

"I haven't figured it out—yet. For now we're just having fun together."

"Fun is all you need from a dog."

The following Monday, Miss Kinsky announced exploring the graves as the class project.

Saturday morning students in jeans, sweatshirts, and light jackets gathered near the school bus for the half-day event.

As Gary's mom dropped him off, Tom yelled, "Where's Pepper?"

"Mom wouldn't let me bring him."

The custodian Bill followed the bus in a gray pickup truck loaded with garden tools. Fifteen minutes later they parked on the side of a dirt road near Fryer Lane.

Miss Kinsky put on a wide-brimmed orange cloth hat. "I'll be checking to make sure there's no running around or disappearing in the woods. We're here to gather information and you'll be graded on your efforts. Don't disrespect the graves, and bring me anything you find. I'll tag it for our records." She slid on heavy work gloves. "Now let's get started."

Bill shoved a wheelbarrow over the narrow dirt path followed by Miss Kinsky and eighteen students with rakes, shovels, and other tools. Behind them two parent volunteers pushed a cart loaded with canned beverages and a metal detector.

When the path ended, Bill turned to Miss Kinsky. "The site is a couple hundred yards ahead through those bushes, trees, and thick vines." He pointed. "Careful—that's poison ivy."

Miss Kinsky adjusted her hat. "No wonder it's been hidden all these years." She signaled for Gary and some of the other boys to come forward. "We need a path cleared. Make it wide enough to walk two abreast and pull the wheel barrels through. And watch yourselves with those sharp metal tools."

Perched on a low branch of an oak tree about thirty feet away, a large gray squirrel stared at Miss Kinsky. It bolted toward a stand of white mulberry trees after the boys began swinging their garden tools.

Gary and Tom cut and chopped through vegetation. Others raked debris and tossed branches and small logs to the side. Thirty minutes later they arrived at the site.

Gary ran and placed his hand on Sarah's headstone. "She was our age when she died."

"I wonder what killed her," Judy said.

Students removed bushes and raked undergrowth exposing a total of nine graves.

"These granite headstones must have come from that quarry," Miss Kinsky said.

The two rows of graves covered about two hundred square-feet, bordered by large oaks and sixty-foot red maples. Bill figured some of those trees were a hundred years old.

Miss Kinsky catalogued names and birth/death dates while one of the parents swept the cleared area with a metal detector. They discovered nails, a belt buckle, and a horse shoe. Bill focused his Polaroid camera and snapped pictures of the items then Miss Kinsky wrapped them in white cloth and placed them in a shoe box.

A red fox curled under a buttonbush snarled at a couple of Gary's buddies. They tossed a few rocks and it bolted down the hill taking cover in a dense patch of yellow ferns.

A large hawk displayed its bold-white chest feathers as it circled the group.

Tom glanced up. "Think he knows why we're here?"

"Ask him," Gary said.

Judy waved Miss Kinsky over and pointed to a line of rocks and gravel pushing a few inches above the grass. "What about this?"

"It might be an old foundation wall," Miss Kinsky responded.

Around eleven-thirty, Miss Kinsky called the group together. "I don't want souvenir hunters disturbing the site. So tell your friends to stay away. In a few weeks, I'll schedule another trip out here."

She signaled Judy to step forward. "Let's thank your classmate for discovering what might be what's left of these folks' home or barn?"

"None of us would be here if it wasn't for Gary…and his dog Pepper," Tom yelled.

"It ain't even his dog," Judy responded.

Miss Kinsky glanced at Tom. "We all own this project." She reached into one of the wheelbarrows and grabbed a handful of wooden posts with small red flags and handed them to Bill. "Mark off an area a little beyond where we've explored. The posts have the village logo on them. That'll keep people from disturbing the site."

"He's still watching," Tom said.

Gary waved at the hawk perched atop an oak tree twenty yards away. "It's his turf."

They headed back a little before twelve o'clock circling around gullies and patches of poison ivy.

As they passed a stand of long-needled Scotch Pines, Tom said, "I love the smell of pines. Let's get back in early December and cut a few to sell for Christmas trees."

"Nah, I got a feeling we shouldn't disturb this place too much," Gary said.

Just beyond the pine trees, Judy dragged her rake over a bumble bee nest. Bees poured out and everyone ran like hell. Miss Kinsky's big orange hat flew off while she scrambled toward the bus.

At the bus, Miss Kinsky asked, "Did anybody get stung?"

"I fell and scratched my knee," Sandy cried.

"We'll clean it with alcohol and put a Band-Aid on it when we get back."

Gary whispered to Tom, "What a bunch of babies. I'll bet the folks buried back there didn't run from crap like this."

Bill approached Miss Kinsky. "They dropped a couple of tools on the path."

"We'll get them the next time we're out here," she replied.

After everyone was back on the bus, Miss Kinsky faced her students. "We'll review what we found and figure our next steps. Remember, don't come out here and disturb things—this is a class project."

The following Wednesday, Miss Kinsky stood at the blackboard. "We're naming our project *Lost and Found in Glasgo*w and Pepper will be included in our team photo."

"What if the real owner of that dog shows up before then?" Judy asked.

"Let's not worry about that."

Gary yelled across the room, "No one's taking my dog!"

"Dr. James Best, a local historian and archeologist will date the items we found to see if they match the time periods of the graves. But our biggest challenge is finding out who these people were," Miss Kinsky said.

She looked at Gary. "You and Tom check out the history of the old quarry. Those headstones had to be mined there. There are a couple of retirees from the quarry still around here that might be able to help."

Judy and Samantha would research the library. Others would check with Father Stoeckel, pastor of St. Pius X, regarding any old birth/death records of folks that might be descendants of those buried at the site. Assignments also included calls to the Missouri Historical Society and record checks with local governments in the surrounding counties.

A month later, Miss Kinsky pointed to the horseshoes and belt buckle displayed on a large metal folding table at the front of the classroom. "Dr. Best confirms the items found at the site date to the period of the graves. The oldest grave runs from 1735 to 1795, which belonged to a Phillip Parker. Maybe he spent most of his life somewhere else, but we know he was here by 1795. The last death date showed 1860. That's at least sixty-five years these folks raised and hunted food and dealt with whatever came their way. It's a shame we haven't discovered who they were. Property and death records were sparse around here prior to 1860. But maybe we'll find something."

She held up a photo. "See the foundation wall. Dr. Best has agreed to come along and examine that area when we go back in November."

"I discovered that wall," Judy shouted.

Gary tapped Tom on the shoulder. "Remember that dead mouse we saw outside the gym?"

"Yeah."

"Let's toss it in front of that loud mouth's locker."

"How about dropping it on her desk?"

"Even better."

After school Gary stopped at the grocery and bought a softball-sized red spongy ball and a bag of beef-flavored doggie treats.

When he got home, Gary tossed the ball into the backyard. "Here, Pep, a new toy."

Pepper ran to the fence to show it to the neighbor's golden retriever then scurried back to drop it at Gary's feet. Gary handed Pepper a doggie biscuit and they settled under the willow tree.

Dr. Best, short and chubby, in brown baggy pants and safari hat, waved as the school bus pulled up that second Saturday in November. Miss Kinsky introduced Dr. Best and reminded everyone whatever they found must be turned over to her. They recovered the rakes dropped from before, but no sign of bumble bees.

Tom nudged Gary as they walked along the path. "Have you seen that hawk around?"

"Nope, he must've headed south."

Dr. Best had perimeter markers expanded by fifty feet. The parent with the metal detector scanned those areas while Dr. Best studied what appeared to be remnants of a foundation.

Gary spotted an orange hat just outside the new perimeter and approached Miss Kinsky. "Hey, there's your hat by that maple tree. Want me to go get it?"

"I've already bought another. Forget about it. Go see if Dr. Best needs help."

Two hours later, Miss Kinsky gathered the group. "Dr. Best is convinced the foundation is probably what's left of these folks' home. We picked up another old horseshoe he believes to be from a barn area. The mayor told me they had planned on zoning this for an industrial park. Our discovery changed that. Now it'll be a nature preserve with the graves maintained by the city. Also, the *Glasgow Village News* will publish a front page story with pictures about what we discovered." The students erupted with claps and cheers.

Tom put his hand on Gary's shoulder. "We can thank my buddy…and his dog."

While boarding the bus, Gary whispered to Tom, "I'm going to get Miss Kinsky's hat."

"What the hell for?"

"I'll hang it in my room. It'll be neat to have."

"You're crazy!"

When he got home, Gary spotted his sisters in the backyard clapping while Pepper raced between them clutching his new ball.

He swung open the gate. "Quit bothering my dog."

"He ain't just your dog. We got a right to have fun with him," Pat shouted.

"I bought him that toy."

"So what, it's his toy," his sister insisted. "He wanted to come out and play."

Pepper grabbed his red ball and ran under the willow tree.

"Look at him—he's having fun. Stop being a jerk."

Mom pushed open the back door. "It's time for lunch."

Pepper beat everyone through the door.

The following Monday, Gary asked Tom, "What happened?"

Tom touched a large bruise under his right eye. "That big fat creep picked a fight outside the dime store."

"You mean Buster? He's got twenty pounds on you."

"He ain't so tough. It was a pretty good fight until the owner of the dime store stopped it. I was winning—I think."

"You never know till it's over."

After reciting the Pledge, Miss Kinsky looked at Tom. "Did that happen at school?"

"Nope, up at the store."

She shook her head. "Next Monday, folks at the *Glasgow Village News* are going to take our class picture for the December issue. We'll appear on the front page along with pictures of the gravesite and the items we found. They're doing a story about the work we've done bringing this part of Glasgow Village history to life."

"What about my dog Pepper?" Gary asked.

"Have your mom bring him in Monday; we'd all like to meet this wonder dog of yours. He'll be in front for the photo. I'll make sure his role is included in the write-up. Folks will love that."

Tom turned to Gary. "Aren't you worried the real owners might see the picture and want their dog back?"

"He's mine. No one's taking him."

Early Saturday, Gary answered a knock at the front door. It was an old woman he and Tom interviewed for the project.

"Remember me, young man?" she said.

"Yes, your name is . . . Margaret. You used to work at the quarry."

"I phoned but nobody answered."

Gary introduced her to his parents and then he and Margaret sat on the couch.

She held up a tattered old book. "You asked for information about people buried in those woods near the quarry. This will help."

She turned a few pages. "After you and Tom left, I paged through a bunch of old books they gave me when I retired from the quarry. This lay at the bottom of a stack in my basement. It's a journal written by folks named Dunham and Parker. The dates match the time periods you mentioned."

"That's them. What does it say?"

"It tells where they came from, the challenges they faced, and how they made their living. There's one particular tragedy that devastated them. How a young girl named Sarah died."

Gary nodded. "I've seen her grave!"

She handed Gary the book. "You keep this. Some of the pages are faded but you shouldn't have trouble reading it."

"Margaret, would you like a cup of coffee?" Gary's mom asked.

"Thanks, but no. I've got to run to the grocery. The radio says we'll get snow tomorrow. I hate driving in that stuff."

After Margaret left, Gary put the book on his dresser, grabbed his coat and headed out the door.

"Where are you going?" his mom asked.

"I'll be back in a couple of hours."

With snow on the way, Gary wanted to get that orange hat before it disappeared.

Twenty minutes later, cold air swept his face as he hurried past the gravesites. His trophy lay in a small depression half buried in a pile of leaves just beyond the area they had searched.

Gary grabbed the hat and pulled it down over his head. When he turned to leave something sharp poked the bottom of his tennis shoe. After clearing away leaves and dirt it turned out to be a bracelet. He shoved it in his pocket and hurried home.

When Gary walked through the front door, his mom yelled, "Take that dirty, stupid thing off your head."

"You like it?" Gary responded.

"Did you pull that out of a dumpster?"

"Nope, it belonged to Miss Kinsky. She doesn't want it."

"Why do you have it?"

"It got blown off her head at the gravesite. I just picked it up."

"Wash your hair, and don't let your dad see you wearing that."

Gary flung the hat on his dresser next to the journal, dropped the bracelet inside a drawer, and then headed to the bathroom.

After lunch, Gary opened the journal while Pepper sat at the end of his bed staring at the dresser drawer.

The journal told how two farm families named Dunham and Parker traveled west in 1785 from the Carolinas settling not far from the quarry. Passages described building the cabin, hunting deer, going hungry during winters, celebrating Christmas, and trading with Indians from across the big river which Gary figured had to be the nearby Mississippi.

About a third way through Gary found the section about the death of twelve-year-old Sarah Dunham. It described how she and her dog were playing on the ice of a small pond near the cabin when the ice broke. Both died and were buried together with Sarah cradling her dog Skippy.

Gary set the book down and washed the bracelet off in the bathroom sink. In faint letters was the name Sarah Dunham.

Gary rushed to the living room and handed the bracelet to his mom. "This belonged to that twelve-year-old girl buried up at the gravesites. She drowned with her dog. Maybe that's how she lost the bracelet?"

"Miss Kinsky will be thrilled. The tragedy of the little girl and her dog is a story in itself."

"I'll surprise the class on Monday with all this new information. It'll be fun."

She handed the bracelet back. "That poor girl—so young."

Gary glanced at Pepper. "And that poor dog."

Driving home from Sunday services, Gary's dad glanced at his wife. "It's starting to snow. I'll have to get those snow tires out of the garage." He flipped on the window wipers. "I'll put them on later this morning. It shouldn't take long."

"Gary, help your dad with that," Mom said.

"Sure, Mom."

Around ten-thirty, Gary was reading the journal when his mom shouted from the living room. "Your dad wants you out in the garage."

"I'll be right there." He put the journal down on the bed and looked at Pepper. "We're wrapping up our project on those gravesites and you get to be in the team picture." He tossed the bracelet on top of the dresser and left.

After examining the tires, his dad decided to buy a new set at Sears the following Saturday.

Gary discovered the bracelet gone when he got back to his room.

He confronted his sisters. "Who took the bracelet?"

"We ain't got it," Pat replied. "Maybe Mom is looking at it?"

He ran to the kitchen. "Mom, have you seen that bracelet I found?"

"Not since I handed it back to you."

He searched his room again, and then said. "Mom, where's Pepper?"

"I let him out about ten minutes ago. He was scratching at the back door with something in his mouth—probably a doggie biscuit. Why don't you call him in?"

He opened the door. "Hey, Pep." The neighbor's golden retriever barked a few times, but no Pepper.

He turned to his mom. "Are you sure somebody didn't let him in?"

"I've been in the kitchen the whole time. He must be out there."

From the porch, he spotted snowy paw prints heading through the open gate. "Some idiot left the gate open. I have to get him before he's hit by a car or freezes."

He threw on his tan leather coat, grabbed Pepper's green sweater from the closet, and yelled at his sisters to come up with the bracelet.

Pepper's prints tracked down the driveway, crossed the street, turned at the corner, and then continued across an area graded for new homes.

He saw Pepper in the distance heading across an open field. Racing to close the gap he stumbled and fell face first into the snow. When he looked up Pepper had disappeared, but his tracks led into the woods.

The snowy paw prints zig-zagged through leaf-filled gullies and around trees ending at Sarah Dunham's grave—but no tracks or signs of Pepper beyond that.

At the quarry, all he found were a couple of loud Canada geese. Running toward a bush he tripped and slid down a snow-packed hill. Wet and cold, he chased every sound and movement in the surrounding woods.

After thirty minutes, eyes watering and exhausted, Gary faced Sarah's grave. "He was happy with us. We planned on surprising him with his own dog house next spring. Come Monday, he's going to be in our class picture. Why not let him go?"

After a prayer, he put his hand on Sarah's gravestone. "I'm glad you got your bracelet back." He laid the green sweater on the grave. "If he gets cold make him wear it." He walked a few feet and turned. "Tell him I'm bringing his red ball next time I come."

Gary leaned against the porch banister watching snow cover his bike.

His mom opened the kitchen door. "Where's Pepper?"
"He's back with his first family."
Pat shouted from the doorway, "You let them take him!"
Gary wiped away a tear. "I couldn't do anything."
"Too bad, I loved having him around," his mom said.
"I can visit him whenever I want."

His mom stepped onto the porch. "Who are the owners? Do we know them?"

"I guess in a way."

"What's his real name?"

"They called him Skippy, but he's Pepper to me."

"Are they gonna let him pose with the class on Monday?"

"I don't think so."

"That's a shame. Maybe Miss Kinsky can call and explain."

"That wouldn't do any good."

"We'll all miss him, but we knew he belonged to someone else."

"Mom—I don't think he wanted to go back. He was happy here."

She headed inside. "Come in before you catch a cold."

Gary spotted Pepper's red ball under the willow tree. "I'll be just a minute."

Pat stuck her head out the door. "I'm going next time you visit."

Gary's mom interrupted. "We'll all go visit him before Christmas."

"He'd like that," Gary said.

As Gary walked toward the willow tree, his sister crowed, "What about that bracelet?"

Gary squeezed the spongy red ball. "It's back with its owner."

Next Stop Wunderland

David tapped his mom's shoulder. "How long before we get there?"

She glanced back. "It will be another fifteen or twenty minutes. And keep your big mouth shut while we're there. Remember what happened to your Aunt Jane and Uncle Bill on their visit. We ain't heard from them in six months. Be careful!"

"Aw, Mom, nobody cares about a skinny runt like me."

David's dad swung the steering wheel to avoid a squirrel darting across the road. "They keep watch on everyone—even fourteen-year-olds like yourself. All it takes is a careless word."

David grabbed the collar of his white shirt. "This stupid tie makes me feel like I'm being strangled."

"Shut up," his mom yelled.

David brushed back his light-brown hair, inhaled the faint smell of burning leaves, and wished he was somewhere else.

The twenty-year-old silver Jeep sped past the fall leaves blown in heaps or clinging to treetops along the dusty road. Temperature on the dash read sixty degrees—perfect sweater weather for mid-October. A doe snuggled next to its fawn as they passed a stand of poplar trees.

Every five years, citizens over the age of ten had to visit their local Wunderland Park on a day designated by the Leadership. These parks had sprung up in every state as part of the first five-year re-education plan. John and Barb Smith, along with son David, had received their attendance notice for this Sunday. Ignoring the notice was a crime.

From over a mile away, David caught sight of the giant neon sign flashing its bright gold WELCOME TO WUNDERLAND

PARK. Surrounding the park stood a ten-foot chain linked fence barbed at the top to prevent people from climbing out. Six lanes kept lines moving as cars arrived.

David's dad presented their photo IDs to bearded characters known as Guardian Angels dressed in black uniforms, black boots, and long blue scarves.

With papers in order, they parked between a rusty pickup truck and silver Mercedes and found themselves with hundreds of elbowing, faceless adults, some hauling noisy kids or cranky seniors, dressed in faded whites, tans, with a spot of color here and there. The Wunderland symbol "WWW" showed bright red on buildings, clothing, cars, and products of every sort.

David tugged on his mom's arm. "What are they doing to those old ladies?" Guardian Angels had shoved three old women toward a two-story metal building. One screamed, while the other two lowered their heads.

His mom pointed at the women. "They're getting what they deserve. The Guardian Angels know what they're doing."

"What happens in that building?" David asked.

A guy passing by, said, "Kid, they yank their truth out of you in there."

David turned, as the man disappeared into the crowd.

The day's formal activities began inside a thousand-seat auditorium. Pitched on a slight hill, its wood plank outer wall was painted gray, much of it peeling. The tan shingled roof showed wear, with tiles flapping with each gust of wind. David imagined it a big barn well past its prime. Inside the walls and floor smelled like they had been soaked in alcohol, causing David's eyes to water and itch as his mom and dad scrambled to get seats in the front row.

At ten o'clock, a middle-aged thick-necked man in tan khaki pants and short sleeve black shirt walked to the podium rubbing his fat hairy chin. "I'm Marduk."

David's mom clapped, which escalated into a chant "Long Live Marduk."

After his father elbowed him, David joined in with everyone else.

When the applause ended, David's mom leaned over. "It's important to clap first and loudest. And always be the last to stop applauding. They notice things like that."

David shrugged. "Why?"

Marduk pulled up an overhead chart. "We're three years into the current five-year economic plan. The results are tremendous, better than ever."

David's mother jumped up and clapped, others followed.

"I know, I know, we're moving forward. It could have been much better if it hadn't been for wreckers and saboteurs who continue to hold us back."

David's mother shouted, "Death to wreckers! Death to saboteurs!" The rest of the audience picked up the chant.

Marduk tapped the podium a couple of times. "Through our diligence, and the alertness of loyal citizens, many of these enemies have been identified."

Marduk signaled, and a fat, red-headed youth in white shirt and gray slacks walked to the center of the stage.

Marduk pinned the prized Gold Eagle on the boy. "His name is Christopher Bullins. He earned the Hero of Security award. At the age of ten, Christopher showed a dedication and willingness many adults and children fail to achieve. He observed, listened, took notes, and delivered evidence of treason to his local Guardian Angel. He spoke at their sentencing—demanding his parents' death. That's the kind of moral strength Wunderland expects from everyone."

Marduk pointed at the audience. "Are you willing to do what's necessary?"

The packed auditorium responded, "Yes!"

"Could you turn in treasonous colleagues, friends, or neighbors?"

"Yes!" the crowd roared.

"Could you turn in your treasonous aunts, uncles . . . even parents?"

"Yes, yes!"

"Could you turn in your treasonous children?"

David listened to his mom shout, "Yes, yes, yes."

"Is there any treasonous person you wouldn't turn in?"

"NO!"

"Have you made your commitment to WUNDERLAND?"

The building shook with, "YES!"

Marduk grinned. "After thirty years of marriage with three children, I didn't hesitate to turn in my wife and eldest daughter when they talked treason."

David twisted in his chair, looked at his mom and dad, and then glanced at the exit sign.

Marduk ordered everyone to sign on to the government site when they got home to study the sections on banned words, banned authors, banned music, banned slogans, banned clothing, banned belief systems, banned facial expressions, banned toys, banned heroes, banned travel locations, banned jokes, banned art, banned opinions, and so on.

Marduk gripped the podium. "You have twenty-four hours to get that done. Then take the online test to measure how well the information has affected your ability to think like a Wunderland citizen. Results are evaluated by the Department of Supreme Justice." He spent the next fifteen minutes reviewing the citizen list of obligations, stressing the importance of being watchful and vigilant.

Marduk closed with the statement, "Don't fail Wunderland."

David and his father hurried toward the crowded exit, while his mom held back, studying a nearby man and woman.

When David's mom emerged, she pointed at a young couple. "Wait here while I report them."

David looked to his father. "What did they do?"

"Who knows? It could be anything, or nothing."

A five-minute walk from the auditorium brought David and his parents to the museum of smashed idols and ideas. Divided by category, visitors toured broken and graffiti-covered statues of past political leaders, sports heroes, scientists, artists, poets, religious figures along with the symbols of those religions including holiday traditions. No captions were provided. Being here was proof they didn't serve Wunderland.

     David knew little of these so-called bad people and traditions since most had been erased from books, teaching, and other sources of communication he had access to. If one of their names did come up at school, it was always in derisive terms.

     As they exited the building, David overheard his mom whisper to his dad. "Did you notice the broken bust of the poet Pushkin? They must have just added him. I've been reading his poetry for years."

     "It was only a matter of time with Pushkin. I'm surprised it didn't happen earlier," he replied.

     "As soon as we get home, I'll purge my computer files. Don't tell anyone I've been a fan."

     "You should've been more careful."

The day's agenda included crossing the Loveless Bridge. The bridge ran five hundred feet above a flat grassy area the size of two football fields. Every half hour, a guide led groups over the bridge while below hundreds of men and women stood in loose-fitting faded-yellow shirts and pants, with orange stocking caps pulled over their shaved heads.

     At one o'clock, David and his parents joined the next group waiting to cross the bridge.

     A slim twenty-something woman named Ashley, wielding a bullhorn, said, "Listen, observe, and learn." A siren wailed for fifteen seconds, causing the people below to come to attention, arms at their sides.

     She stopped the group halfway across the bridge. "What do you see down there? They're young, old, smart, dumb, misfits and losers. All are criminal traitors, wreckers, and saboteurs of our glorious plans. Wunderland has no place or use for them."

She shouted into the bullhorn. "Lawrence Jefferson—remove your cap and step forward."

Pointing, she said, "Six months ago that old man stood up here, taking the tour, leaning against the same railing you are. Now look at him. Get on your knees, traitor." Ashley then described Jefferson's various political and economic crimes as he hung his head.

David spotted Jerry and Pete, a couple of friends from school, and the three of them wandered a short distance from the group.

David turned to Jerry. "How bad do you think they are?"

"You mean the folks down there, or the jerks running this fucking tour?"

"Yeah, it's hard to know the good guys."

"What good guys? Name them," Jerry said.

"Anything we say stays with us," Pete insisted.

David agreed. "I think my mom could sell me out for a bump in her Wunderland report card."

Jerry whispered, "It's a damn shame—the world they built for us. Managed by people who think they're right all the time. I wonder how that feels."

"It must feel damn good, as long as you're in charge," David said in a tight voice.

Jerry shrugged. "It wasn't always like this. People used to be able to think how they wanted to think, say what they wanted to say, go where or when they wanted to go. They even decided who ran things. They called it voting. It's true—there's proof. I've got old paper books that tell about it and a lot more."

"That sounds crazy. How did you get those books?" Pete asked.

"Six weeks ago, I was in the woods near my house. I go there to be alone with my thoughts without people wondering what I'm thinking."

Jerry glanced at the group huddled around Ashley. "I'm lying in the grass and whenever the wind picked up I hear this echo like an angry voice twisting through a long tunnel. The sound came from behind a bunch of overgrown snowball bushes and evergreens."

"That's spooky," David said.

"It sounded like someone calling or trying to reach out to me."

Pete said, "I would have gotten the hell out of there. Weren't you afraid it might be the boogeyman?"

"No such thing as boogeymen, just men." Jerry recalled. "Anyway, I grabbed a stick to beat back the thick growth of vegetation, and discovered an entrance to a cave."

"Damn, what then?" Pete asked.

"I ran home to get a lantern and small shovel. Twenty minutes later, after widening the entrance a little, I crawled inside. I haven't told anyone about the cave."

A woman's shout drew the boys' attention. They watched a short, heavy-set lady leaning over the side of the bridge, cursing at those below.

"That's my mom. She thinks stuff like that scores points with the powers running this show. She's hard core," David said.

Jerry shook his head. "That's their world. It don't have to be ours."

"What about those books?" Pete asked.

"The cave was crammed with dozens of big metal cases. I hoped they contained hidden treasure, and in a way they did. I set the lantern next to one, and found it loaded with old-fashioned paper-bound books with authors named Solzhenitsyn, Orwell, Aristotle, J. S. Mill, plus others. You guys ever hear those names at school, or mentioned by your parents?"

"Nope," Pete said.

"A guy named George Orwell came up during the smashed idols tour," David said.

Jerry continued. "The cave is plenty big to stand in. It goes back hundreds of feet. The next time, I brought a sandwich along with my dad's lantern. A lot of the books are fragile. It felt like discovering sacred texts from long ago. They described a world and approach to life we've never heard of. People sang, shared ideas, and could be happy in public without being viewed as suspicious. I got home after dark, and missed supper. But it was worth it."

"Where did those books come from?" David asked.

"A diary wrapped in plastic lay on top of one of the cases. It belonged to a Jasmine Strong. The last entry was fifty years ago. She said the books were stashed by her rescue team because they contained thoughts, ideas, beliefs, histories, and works of people considered dangerous to the new way. She hoped, if found by virtuous people, they could help reawaken peoples' pursuit of truth and beauty. I couldn't find her name on the Internet. She must have been a real fighter. I'd like to know more about her."

"Yeah, sure, but be careful with Internet searches. They track that shit," Pete warned.

David grabbed Jerry by the arm. "I've got to see those books. It sounds like we've missed so much."

Jerry stammered, "What if your mom found out? Would she turn me in? I don't want my ass dragged below the bridge with those other orange-capped losers."

"She'd turn us all in. I'm not sure about my dad. But they ain't going to find out—I'll never tell."

Jerry pulled Pete and David in close. "Let's meet at my house next Saturday afternoon. We'll head over to the cave and dive into that material. Maybe we can reawaken folks to ideas nobody's heard."

Jerry glanced over at the group. "We're talking treason, so don't tell anyone about our plans."

"What about your crazy little sister, Becca? What if she follows us?" Pete looked apprehensive.

"She doesn't know shit about this. Plus, she's afraid of the woods."

After Jerry agreed to bring the lanterns, Pete the sandwiches and cigarettes, and David the pens and pads of papers, they shook hands and swore an oath of secrecy.

David noticed his mom waving him over. "I got to go. It's next Saturday for sure."

David's mom walked him a little ways from the group, and said, "What did you guys talk about? Did they mention their parents, or other relatives? You know things they might have overheard someone say."

"We just talked school and sports."

"What about that damn hand shaking?"

"They're just old friends. They've both been by the house. You've met them."

"Hand shaking draws attention," his father said. "That's how folks get in trouble."

"I'll be careful."

"Are you sure they didn't tell you stuff I should know about? It could be a small thing like a name mentioned, or something their parents said in anger against Wunderland. Think real hard."

"Nothing, Mom."

"You're no help…neither is your dad."

She shoved David toward the edge of the bridge. "Keep it up, and you'll end up getting your ass beat with those maggots and worms down there. Most of them won't be around a year from now."

Ashley continued calling people to acknowledge their crimes. One old woman, David figured she had to be at least eighty, confessed to hoarding food and extra toilet paper for her invalid husband. A guy named Christopher got caught on camera not clapping in the Leader's presence.

To close the presentation, Ashley had a fourteen-year-old named Jason Tremble confess to reading contraband material. His classmates turned him in. "Jason will be lucky if he's out by the age of twenty-one. You're never too young to learn the right path, or be held accountable when you stray."

As they exited the bridge, David noticed his dad slipping a folded piece of paper to a Guardian Angel.

The final leg of the day's journey included the so-called "fallen angels." These were individuals once held in high esteem by

Wunderland but now condemned for the worst transgression of all—impiety. Given their former prominence, their executions took place before hundreds of spectators to demonstrate no one stood above or beyond the reach of Wunderland justice.

The first execution began at ten o'clock in the morning, followed by another at two in the afternoon. Individuals were placed on a metal platform that jutted fifty feet from the cliff edge, held in place by steel cables. Below the platform lay a thousand foot drop to jagged rocks and boulders. At the designated time, the condemned were expected to jump to their deaths. If an individual refused, the supporting steel cables would be loosened; the platform would then collapse to a vertical position, hurtling them downward. The condemned were permitted a final statement, followed by a brief Wunderland response.

Experiencing an execution was an important right-of-passage in a citizen's life. His parents had been to a half-dozen, but this would be David's first.

For the best views, youth plus first-time spectators were encouraged to gather at the fenced railing around the cliff's edge. Behind that lay ten elevated rows of bleacher seating. First-row seats were for handicapped, Wunderland dignitaries, and college students on school assignments.

While his parents took seats in the bleachers, David ran to the crowded railing section and stared at the gray-haired, frail-looking man with thick glasses on the metal platform. The brochure showed his name as Justin O'Connor, aged forty-eight, former professor of literature, married, and father of four. He was guilty of writing, speaking, and spreading impious thought. Conviction in those areas always led to public execution. His two youngest children, girls aged twelve and fourteen, were announced and then seated in the first row. His wife waited in a nearby prison.

Vendors pitched beer and soda sales while folks, stacked in rows, stretched to get better views. Teenagers and adults laughed and hurled profanities at the man on the platform. They knew their duty—celebrate a righteous execution.

David squeezed the metal railing, and wished he could help that man out there.

At five minutes before two o'clock, a tall, lean man with shoulder-length brown hair and pockmarked face shoved his way past David.

Gripping a microphone, he said, "My name is Igor Kratz."

Kratz glanced at the prisoner O'Connor. "We're here to learn, and make the most of this important exercise. This morning was a big disappointment. Cathy Philips, a car industry executive, offered no apology for her crimes. All we got was damn tears. When the time came, people yelled 'jump.' But she just sat there pleading; her long red hair draped over her eyes. We had to shake her skinny ass loose by relaxing the cables. She got booed all the way down."

David spotted her bloody corpse wedged between two large rocks.

Kratz took a drink of beer from a plastic cup, and said, "This guy, O'Connor, had every Wunderland advantage: great schooling, a job at the best university, good home, nice car, plenty to eat, and respected by many. He had a perfect Wunderland life. Then last spring he threw it all away. Several professors where he taught stepped forward and told us O'Connor's classroom lectures challenged Wunderland's point of view. He praised dangerous thinkers from the past, and even shared their banned books. His wife is locked up for refusing to give evidence, and we're still looking for several of his former students. This man spat at Wunderland, and encouraged others to do the same. It's all on record—check the brochure."

Kratz shrugged. "It doesn't make sense. Yet, here we are. Everybody that makes it to that platform brings it on themselves. Wunderland doesn't want this, but its way of life will be preserved."

Kratz held up the arm of a small girl next to David. "It's her future at stake."

The audience cheered, while David stepped away.

Kratz checked the time, and then glanced at the prisoner. "You got five minutes."

O'Connor dusted off his gray prison trousers as he approached the platform microphone.

After a flock of noisy geese passed, he said, "What makes life worth living?"

He lit a cigarette, and said, "Living is freedom to pursue a career, or to travel, or decide what books you want to read, what ideas to believe, discuss, or propose in the public square without fear. Living is having faith in things greater than Wunderland."

He took a drag and continued. "Living is understanding life through your lens rather than the vision of Wunderland elites.

"George Orwell wrote about another Wunderland many years ago. He told of a two plus two equals five world. That's a world where truth is whatever those in charge say it is, regardless of facts. And you better not challenge their truth.

"Wunderlands are worlds of illusions and lies held together with endless suspects, public apologies, confessions, prisons, and executions."

He glanced at the rocks below. "A life must be free to pursue truth wherever it is."

Kratz faced the packed bleachers. "Meaningless words from a man who has run out of time. This isn't complicated. You can sit up here, or dead walk that metal slab—your choice." He pointed to a young woman in the third row. "Stand and tell us which place you prefer."

O'Connor removed his shoes, socks, gray trousers, and shirt, and then clasped his hands. A white dove appeared and circled above the platform.

Kratz shouted, "Now."

O'Connor stepped to the edge of the platform—naked. "Don't fear death, fear a life without truth." Then he jumped.

O'Connor's daughters, their heads bowed, held each other's hands as their father's thin frame slammed against a large boulder.

David gazed at O'Connor's bloody, broken body and committed himself to finding and sharing truth, regardless of the dangers.

At the sound of a gunshot, Kratz said, "The shot to the head. We have to make sure, in case the rocks don't finish the job. It's the merciful thing to do." Then he announced the event over, and wished everyone a safe drive home.

David banged and elbowed his way out, tripping a loud bushy-haired kid along the way.

When he met up with his parents, his mom asked, "Where's your tie?"

He grabbed his collar. "I must have lost it back there."

"How the hell can you lose a tie? She shoved him. "You're so damn careless."

Near the auditorium, David's dad grabbed him by the hand, as two beefy Guardian Angels ran up.

The taller of the two Angels faced David's mom. "Are you the Barbara Smith that lives at 10342 Ross Circle, in Haverton?"

She clutched her purse. "Yes."

"Come with us. We have questions that need answers."

She dropped her purse. "I didn't do anything. I've always been loyal. I love Wunderland. Whoever spoke against me is a liar."

One Guardian scooped up her purse, and sneered, "I'll bet she'll be a screamer." The other agreed as he grabbed her arms and dragged her toward the same metal building David saw those old ladies taken earlier in the day.

David looked at his dad, as his mom disappeared inside the building.

His dad said, "The Guardian Angels know what they're doing. Let's go."

"What about mom?"

"Nothing we can do."

Ten miles from the park, David's dad turned on the headlights and rolled up the windows as glowing embers and charred trees suddenly lined both sides of the road. Smoke choked the air and blackened the sky. "Wow, see how fast things can change. With the dry leaves, all it took was a spark from a careless fool, or done on purpose by saboteurs. Either way, Wunderland will make them pay."

David nodded as they drove around a dead squirrel and smoldering sign that read Thanks for Visiting Wunderland Park.

David's dad looked over. "We'll stop and get a chocolate sundae at Spiro's."

"Nah, I'm not hungry."

After things cleared up, David rolled down the window to let in some fresh air. "I'll be hanging out with Jerry and Pete, next Saturday. We're going to spend the day exploring the woods near their neighborhood."

His dad tapped the steering wheel. "Don't start any fires while you're there; they can be hard to put out. You can't be too careful."

"Don't worry . . . we'll be careful."

A Story Worth Telling

It was early July when a light went out in a small New England town.

    Katie gazed at the fourth-floor corner window. "Everybody runs out of time. I'll miss him and his little white dog," She shaded her eyes and stared up at the brown brick apartment building. "It seemed his lights were on all night."

    "Yeah, whenever I'd be heading home from Clancy's, no matter how late, I'd always see that bright light on even at one or two in the morning." Nick said.

    "Everybody says he liked to read and was real smart." She turned to Nick. "What was his name?"

    "David something. I know the dog's name was Sparky."

    "What'd he die of…heart attack?"

    "He was overweight and liked to smoke cigars." Nick leaned against the lamppost. "He had a great smile and always waved from across the street when we passed. And what a big deep laugh he had. He lived alone and I believe he attended that church at Shepley and Spring Garden."

    "Saint Paul's?"

    "That's it."

    "I wonder who's taking care of his dog. When I was eight I had a dog that just disappeared one day. I cried, prayed, and cried. I still think about him now and then." She started across the street. "Let's check on the dog."

    Nick and Katie were in their late twenties and had been dating for a couple of months. He worked at a printing shop and owned a small ranch home in town. She lived in a one-bedroom apartment next to the pharmacy where she worked.

Built in 1895, the four-story building had twenty-four apartments, half unoccupied. The twin glass front doors showed small cracks. Bird droppings covered a marble statue of Washington near the entrance.

As they passed the statue, Nick said, "They got to clean that up."

Inside the small lobby they approached a balding old man in jeans holding a black cat.

"Excuse me, did you know the guy that died here recently?" Nick asked.

"You mean Mr. David Tudor. I'm the one that discovered the body and called an ambulance and cops."

"Cops! Was he murdered?" Katie asked.

"I didn't see any blood or bruises. I shook him and he was cold and stiff. He just fell asleep in his big green chair and never woke up. That kinda stuff happens all the time."

"What about his dog?"

"Sparky wouldn't stop barking. I knocked and then went in. I'm the manager and got a pass key to all the apartments." He held up the cat. "This is Freddy."

"Who's taking care of Sparky?"

"I ain't seen him since that day. My guess is the cops took him to the pound or maybe he just ran off." He turned to his cat. "Freddy, do you know where your buddy got off to?"

The old man glanced at Katie. "Would you guys like an apartment? We got plenty available for young couples."

"I wouldn't mind taking a look around. How about showing us the apartment where Mr. Tudor and Sparky lived," she said.

"Mr. Tudor's stuff is still in there. I've got other apartments."

Katie looked over at Nick. "No, it's that fourth-floor view that would interest us."

"I can show it to you, but I'm not sure when it'll be available." The old man set the cat down and pointed. "Let's head up those stairs."

Cracked and scuffed gray floor tiles led to worn wooden steps. Katie whispered to Nick as she gripped the wobbly banister. "Maybe we'll find some clues as to where Sparky has gone."

The walls were covered in dust and the air packed a thick musty smell. At the second-floor landing Nick swatted at a big nasty fly buzzing overhead.

"It's so hot," Katie said.

"The apartments have window air conditioners," the old man said as he fumbled with the keys to unlock the door.

The cat charged in when the door opened a crack, jumped on the green ottoman, sniffed, and then ran into the bedroom.

A small kitchen adjoined a living room/dining area. The dark mahogany bookshelf ran along the wall with overflow books stacked on the floor. Next to the bookshelf sat a large green-clothed easy chair and a small table that held a brass-colored lamp, a bright-red glass ashtray filled with cigar butts, and a framed photo of Sparky.

Katie held her nose. "This room smells."

"I'll open a window," the old man said. "Mr. Tudor had an unlit cigar in his hand and a book about Aristotle in his lap when I found him."

"There are books here on philosophy, history, and poetry." Nick held up two books. "Keats and Marcus Tullius Cicero, that's heavy lifting."

The old man raised the blinds and opened the window. "Mr. Tudor liked his cigars and books. He'd sit in here for good parts of the day reading. I'd stop by sometimes in the evening, he'd pour us a drink, usually scotch, and share what he'd just read. I'll miss him. He was a good man." He turned to Katie. "Take a look at this view. You can see all the way down the block."

The old man smiled as the cat jumped on the ottoman. "This little guy and Sparky would listen to Mr. Tudor read aloud. I have a feeling they understood more than they let on."

"Animals are smarter than people think," Katie said.

"Mr. Tudor told me he taught his dog to read. And the dog helped him write a collection of poems." The old man glanced around the room. "That transcript is around here somewhere."

Nick laughed, and said, "That's hard to believe."

"Mr. Tudor never lied to me."

Nick scanned the bookshelf. "What's happens with these books? I'll bet some are worth a lot of money."

"Mr. Tudor told me he had valuable first editions. I don't know where they'll end up. He never mentioned any close relatives."

"I'd hate to see them end up in some damn flea market. Once the estate gets worked out maybe they'll be donated to a library or sold to collectors who show great books the respect they deserve. Did he leave a will?" Nick asked.

"Don't know."

Katie smiled. "I hope he provided for his dog."

"I'm sure he did," the old man said.

"So where's the dog?" she said.

The old man closed the window and lowered the blinds. "I'd start with the dog pound in case he needs rescuing from that death house. They don't fool around down there. Next I'd check with the pastor at St. Paul's."

Katie grabbed the photo of Sparky. "I'll return this when we find him."

Scooped off the street or donated by their owners, hundreds of dogs including puppies spent their final days at the Eureka dog pound. Located at the far end of town just beyond the railroad tracks the brick building had once been a leather goods and furrier warehouse. Monday through Friday at four in the afternoon white smoke poured from a chimney in the back marking that day's cremation of those unfortunate creatures that'd run out of time.

As they pulled into the pound's parking lot, Nick checked his watch. "Let's make this quick. I want to get out of here before that tower in the back starts puffing its white smoke."

"I cry when that smoke smell gets blown uptown," Katie said.

Nick opened the gray metal door as Katie pulled the photograph of Sparky from her purse.

A young woman in jeans and red flannel shirt rose from behind a small wooden desk. "Are you guys dropping off or looking to adopt?"

"Looking for one in particular," Katie said. She held out the photo. "Have you seen this handsome guy?"

"He looks familiar. But so many animals make their way through here. I lose track."

"How long do you keep an animal?" Nick asked.

"They get checked in and the clock starts ticking. If not claimed they're euthanized two weeks later. How long has your dog been missing?"

Nick shrugged. "It's been ten days or so."

"If we got him he should still be here unless he was injured and had no collar. Then he's disposed of immediately on humanitarian grounds."

"He probably had a collar, but his owner died. We're here to rescue him," Nick said.

"We call the number on the collar and will always leave a message. If we don't hear back within fourteen days…that's it. You guys want to take a look?"

"Yep," Katie said.

Rapid barks and puppy whines poured out as the woman opened a door. "This is where we store the creatures."

Katie held her hands over her ears. "What a sad place."

"You get used to it," the woman said.

Katie shook her head. "Never!"

There were four large metal cages with concrete floors. Urine smells and stink from dog feces filled the room. Some of the animals leaned up against the cage, barked, and tried to make eye contact with Katie and Nick. Others sat motionless at the rear of the cage.

"These guys up front are hoping you'll take them home. I think the guys in the back are resigned to their fate." The woman shrugged. "Most dogs seem to know what's coming."

Katie reached down and petted a whimpering light brown cocker spaniel pressed up against the cage.

"He's six years old. A lady dropped him off a couple of days ago. She was moving and couldn't take him with her. She said his name was Happy. He's very friendly."

Katie teared up. "These poor animals."

"Do you see the dog?"

Nick stared at the photo and then the cages. "He isn't here. Maybe we'll come back in a week or so." He tapped Katie on the shoulder. "We better get going. It's twenty minutes till four."

Katie rubbed Happy's chin and then hurried out the door leaving behind dozens of desperate cries. In the parking lot, she said, "Somebody's got to rescue Happy."

Nick opened the car door. "Tomorrow after work let's check with the pastor. A lot of animals need help. We can't save them all. But I'm rooting for Happy too."

As Nick started up the engine the young woman they had just met waved and approached the car. She leaned against the passenger side door. "I just remembered where I saw that little white dog."

"Great," Katie said.

"About a week ago right here in the parking lot he was barking and growling at people dropping off animals. He scared one lady so much she ran back to her car and took off without leaving the animal. She never did come back."

"Wow, I guess he was doing his own form of rescue," Nick said.

"I think so."

"So what happened?" Katie asked.

"One of our drivers chased after him." She pointed toward a tree-lined road across the street. "He took off over there. I haven't seen him around here since. He had a collar so we figured he ran home. That's all I know."

Katie thanked her and turned to Nick. "Isn't the church in that direction?"

"Sure is."

"Let's run by there tomorrow and ask the pastor if he's seen Sparky."

Tuesday, a little after four o'clock, Nick and Katie pulled into the church lot and parked near an oak tree to catch its late-day shade. The rectory was a small one-story frame building with worn roof shingles and tan siding. Nearby stood the old red-brick church built in 1890.

Crouched next to a red rose bush an old man in jeans and a wide-brimmed straw hat was cutting roses and putting them in a glass vase.

Nick shut the car door, and pointed. "Is that the gardener?"

"I think that's the pastor," Katie said.

The pastor faced Nick and Katie. "Welcome to Saint Paul's. How can I help you?"

Katie smiled, and said, "We're wondering if you've seen a little white dog roaming around."

"You mean Mr. Tudor's dog Sparky?"

"That's him," Nick said.

"Sparky sat in the back of church during Mr. Tudor's funeral mass." The pastor glanced at the church graveyard. "Sparky watched his friend get buried and then sat next to the grave for several days. I brought him food and water, but he wouldn't leave the gravesite. Then one morning I went out with food and he was gone and I haven't seen him since. I've looked around, even checked those woods. "

"Where do you think he might be?" Katie asked. "He's not at the dog pound."

"Good question, he was so loyal to Mr. Tudor. I'm worried that he might be lost without him."

The pastor walked toward a nearby picnic bench. "Let's talk." He placed the vase on the table. "I gave Mr. Tudor that dog. It wandered in here covered in dirt from those woods as a puppy and I sure wasn't going to take it to that pound. I mentioned at the end of a homily that I had a puppy that needed a home and Mr. Tudor stepped forward. He was a fine man and good Christian. He volunteered a lot and always brought Sparky. He claimed the dog wanted to volunteer too and I believe him. I'd love to keep the dog here but the bishop told me he's closing this church next month. I'm headed to a home for retired priests and they don't allow pets."

"If we find him do you think a parishioner would take him in?" Katie asked.

The pastor shook his head. "I asked around with no luck. Most folks don't want to take on the needs of an old dog and Sparky's over fifteen. He'll have trouble surviving on his own."

"I'm worried." Katie glanced at Nick. "We'll take him in."

"Have you guys checked Driscoll's Bar over on Tay Avenue? Mr. Tudor stopped by there with Sparky every Wednesday night for years. Sparky might have run there."

"That'll be our next stop," Nick said.

Katie wrote her telephone number on a piece of paper and handed it to the pastor. "Call if Sparky shows up."

"I'm glad some folks still care." He put the paper in his pocket and then pointed toward the graveyard. "There'll be only one more burial there. When my time comes the bishop promised I could be buried under the shade of that oak tree not far from Mr. Tudor. I've been pastor here over forty years and served communion to a lot of the folks out there."

He handed Katie the vase packed with bright red roses. "Down the road when I'm resting out there feel free to visit. And make sure you check out those woods. There's a great walking path and a stream at one end." He glanced at the woods. "I've seen strange sights out there."

Nick leaned toward the pastor. "What do you mean?"

The pastor scratched his head. "Maybe it's my imagination."

Katie sniffed the roses. "We'll make it by."

Nick glanced back as they walked to the car. "I wonder who's going to take care of the garden when he's gone."

"We will."

"So we're rescuing gardens as well as dogs."

"Sure, it'll be fun."

As they pulled away, Nick said, "Next stop Driscoll's."

Driscoll's was just another neighborhood bar…except Wednesday evenings from seven to nine-thirty when Mr. Tudor and Sparky dropped by.

Wednesday, a little past six-thirty in the evening, Nick and Katie parked across the street and watched the red neon flash Driscoll's.

"We don't have to stay long," Nick said.

Katie nodded. "When I was little my dad used to stop by here after work on Fridays. Mom didn't serve dinner till he got home—usually around eight."

They sat at the end of the bar and a short heavyset man with thick gray hair walked over. "Name's Joe, what can I get you?"

"Two draught beers and information," Nick said.

Katie leaned across the bar. "Have you seen a little white dog around here in the past few days?"

"Are you asking about Mr. Tudor's old dog Sparky?"

"Yep, we're looking for him," Katie said.

Joe smiled as he set the beer mugs on the bar. "That was some dog." He pointed at an empty chair. "He'd sit right there next to Mr. Tudor every Wednesday night between seven and nine thirty." Joe reached under the bar and held up a doggie biscuit. "I'd give him one of these before Mr. Tudor got started."

"Got started?" Nick asked.

Joe gazed at the empty chair and table. "At seven o'clock I'd pour Mr. Tudor a large scotch and water and light his cigar. Then he'd spend the evening talking about science, history, literature…you name it. People crowded around to listen. One week he went on about poet John Keats and recited a beautiful poem titled *To Autumn*. You could tell Keats was his favorite poet. Wednesday was our best and busiest night."

"What'd Sparky do while this was going on?" Katie asked.

"He stared at Mr. Tudor and listened, hardly ever turned his head. I could tell he was getting as much out of the talks as anyone else. That was one smart dog. And the dog was loyal. He'd take an attitude, you know—get feisty—whenever anyone got loud or debated Mr. Tudor about something. That dog would have none of it."

Joe glanced at the wall. "Ten years ago Mr. Tudor showed up with that dog, bought everyone a drink, and they never missed a Wednesday after that. All I got left is memories and that photo I took a couple of years ago of them sitting together at their table. Mr. Tudor smiling with a cigar and Sparky's holding a biscuit in his mouth."

Nick swung around on the bar stool and scanned the half-empty room. "Have you seen the dog since Mr. Tudor passed?"

"Nope, but I wondered where he got off to. Did you ask the pastor?"

"He told us Sparky showed up for the funeral and then disappeared after a couple of days," Katie said. "We checked the pound. They tried to grab him but he got away."

Joe laughed, and said, "Those boobs at the pound would never get Sparky in one of their death cages. He's smarter than them."

The sound of a beer mug being knocked over drew their attention to the end of the bar where two old men were arm wrestling.

Joe glanced down the bar. "The loser has to buy the other guy's beer for the night. Pete hasn't won in ten years."

After Pete's arm went down, Nick turned and said, "Do you think anyone here might know something?"

"Let's ask." Joe slapped the counter several times. "Hey, has anyone seen or know where our friend Sparky is? We're worried he might be in trouble."

There were several shrugs and no's. One woman shouted in a slurred voice, "He hitched a ride out of town."

Joe turned to Nick. "Don't pay any attention to that loudmouth. Sparky would never leave town with Mr. Tudor still here…alive or dead. He's that kind of dog."

"Where do we go from here?" Katie asked.

"I got an idea," Joe said. "I'll organize a search this weekend. Mr. Tudor and Sparky had a lot of friends here. I'm sure they'd be willing to throw in a couple of hours Sunday afternoon walking and driving around searching for Sparky."

"That's great," Katie said. "We'll be there."

"Suppose we find him," Joe said. "What are your plans?"

"We'll adopt him," Katie said.

"That'll be up to Sparky. He's real independent."

"Dogs shouldn't be left to fend for themselves."

"Don't underestimate that dog. He'll figure something out," Joe said.

"I'm praying we find him," Katie said.

Nick put his hand on Katie's shoulder. "Things will work out."

Sunday at noon around twenty people gathered in front of Driscoll's.

Katie addressed the volunteers. "Thanks for agreeing to help locate our friend Sparky. Let's give it a few hours and meet back here around three o'clock." She held up her cellphone. "Send me a picture and video if you spot him."

The group dispersed, some on foot, some on bikes, and others driving to different parts of town. Nick and Katie searched back roads near the church. Nick figured Sparky would want to stay close to Mr. Tudor's grave.

They spotted the pastor loading boxes into the back of a station wagon as they passed the church.

"Looks like he's packing things," Katie said.

"In a few weeks this is gonna be just another place holding memories of days gone. Even that dies out over time," Nick said.

"So sad."

Their phones rang several times with folks letting them know they hadn't spotted Sparky.

Around two o'clock, as they drove past the church, Nick gazed at the nearby woods. "That's where I'd be…if I was Sparky."

"Let's take a quick look," Katie said.

Nick pulled to the side of the road. "Pastor said he already looked, but it's a big space. We might get lucky."

They crossed a grassy field and joined the path which zig zagged through a mix of towering oaks and underbrush packed tight with bushes, tall grass, twisted weeds, vines, and patches of colorful wildflowers.

After forty minutes of looking and shouting Sparky's name, Nick said, "Let's call it a day."

"A couple times I thought I saw something."

"We can always come back for another look."

By three-fifteen everyone had gathered back at Driscoll's. An elderly couple on bikes said they talked to someone who remembered seeing a little white dog rooting through a neighbor's trash can a week earlier.

Katie addressed the group. "Nick and I are putting up a one-hundred dollar reward for information that leads us to Sparky." She held up the photograph of Sparky. "I'll have copies made of this with the reward information and post them around town. Meanwhile keep a lookout and call me or Nick if you see or hear anything."

Thursday morning Katie called the pound to check about Sparky, and then asked if Happy was still there. She left work around two o'clock stopping at a pet shop to pick up canned dog food, a leash, and a water bowl, and then headed to the pound.

Katie pushed open the door and walked to the front desk holding a leash. "I'm here to adopt Happy."

"I remember you from last week. Most of the time they just come and go around here, but Happy is special. I'm glad you came back because he only had a couple days left."

"I know. Don't forget to call me or Nick if that little white dog shows up."

"I will."

Fifteen minutes later Katie left with Happy curled up in the front seat next to her. She called Nick around five o'clock and announced Happy was safe but they needed to find Sparky.

By late September the church had closed and Katie was taking daily walks with Happy around the neighborhood. But no sign of Sparky.

Sunday morning Nick called Katie on the phone. "I just read that Mr. Tudor's estate was settled. He donated those books to the University Library, and the balance, over half-million dollars, went to a No-Kill animal shelter."

"Great to hear more animals will get care they need." She glanced out her apartment window. "Let's drive out to the church and cut a few late blooming roses. I'll bring Happy and we can walk those woods near the church."

"I'll be right over."

Nick scanned the empty church parking lot. "It feels strange; Sunday morning and no cars."

Katie pointed to the graveyard. "Everything moves on."

Katie led Happy toward the garden while Nick brought a clipper and a container.

She smiled, and said, "So lovely, and such sweet aromas. I don't know who planted it originally, probably someone buried out there. But we're taking care of it now. I'm sure no one will object."

Nick held out the plastic container. "I forgot to fill it with water."

"We'll fill it with stream water and cut a few roses when we get back." She glanced down at Happy. "Let's look around."

Katie leaned against a window and gazed inside the empty church. "Think of all the prayers, first communions, and singing that went on in there the last hundred years. Plus parish picnics, fund raisers, and prayer chains." She pointed at the patio. "I imagine that's where they set picnic tables and folding chairs for the Friday fish fries. That's all gone…as if it never happened."

"Like a business, when customer demand for your product falls you close up."

"I was raised in a church just like this. My dad was a deacon."

"I didn't know that," Nick said.

Happy tugged on the leash.

"All right, we'll explore a little," Katie said. "We'll visit the graveyard and then head to the stream and fill that container."

A hundred graves were spread over several acres that butted up against the woods. Weeds had grown around a few of the gravestones.

Nick stared at the graves. "Folks fade away taking their stories with them. It's too bad. I'll bet a lot are real interesting."

"Over here," Katie shouted.

She knelt next to Mr. Tudor's grave and pointed to a short phrase under his name. "It's in Latin, and says, 'A room without books is like a body without a soul.' It's a quote from Cicero." She glanced up at Nick. "I'd like to know more about Mr. Tudor."

"We've learned a little over the last couple of months." Nick laughed. "Maybe we'll ask Sparky to fill in more details if he ever shows up."

"Last night I dreamt we were driving near here and there was Sparky walking on the side of the road. We pulled over and I opened the car door and asked him to jump in. He approached until a man's voice called out and he turned and disappeared." She rose, and said, "It seemed so real."

Happy began to bark.

"Something's got him all excited. Maybe Sparky's over there in the woods," Katie said.

"It's been months since anyone has seen him. More likely it's a squirrel or rabbit."

With Happy tugging on the leash, they walked into the woods.

"We'll stick to the path. I don't want Happy roaming or chasing after things in there."

They stepped around a big box turtle munching a June bug and then spooked a cottontail that darted into a patch of purple wildflowers. Happy's ears perked up when a breeze pushed crackling dry leaves across the path.

"Did you hear that?" Katie said.

"The rustle from a few leaves."

"No, no, no…it was the sound of a dog barking." She pointed to the right. "Over there. Happy heard it."

"All I hear is the stream."

"Let's hurry."

Katie and Happy jumped over a log that had fallen across the path and started to run. Happy barked and pulled hard on the leash. At the stream… nothing but the soft sound of water flowing over and around rocks and lapping the muddy bank. They stared up and downstream.

Nick scooped the plastic container into the water. "I don't see any fresh paw prints or other animal tracks."

"I heard it and so did Happy."

"Then it was probably a fox. A dog, especially an old one, couldn't survive very long in the woods. That's just the way it is."

"Then you wait here. I'm gonna check this out. I'll be back in a few minutes."

Nick tossed a rock into the stream and sat down. "OK, shout if you need me."

Katie nodded. "Come on Happy, let's go."

A minute later they were out of Nick's sight.

The stream bordered the path on the left for a few hundred more yards and then the path swung into the thickest part of the woods where it was bounded on both sides by tall oaks screening much of the sunlight. Damp leaves from a light drizzle the night before enhanced the surrounding late-summer woodsy smells.

Katie stopped to admire a small patch of deep-blue wildflowers waving in a field of green when Happy began barking.

"What's up, boy?" Katie said.

Just off the path in a clearing about fifty yards away stood a small white dog next to a man with a book under his arm smoking a cigar.

"Damn, that's Sparky and Mr. Tudor," she yelled as she ran toward the pair.

The man smiled and waved and then he and the dog disappeared into a glowing silver mist.

Katie hurried to the grassy clearing where Happy sniffed around and discovered a cigar butt.

Twenty minutes later, Katie waved and ran toward Nick still sitting next to the stream. "You won't believe this!"

"Another minute and I was coming to look for you."

"I found Sparky!"

Nick got up. "What! Why didn't you bring him back? Did he run off?"

"He was with someone and they both looked fine." She glanced down at Happy. "I've thought about it on the way back. I'm sure it was Mr. Tudor. He smiled at me, took a puff on his cigar, and then disappeared into a mist with Sparky. Happy saw it too."

"Show me where."

"They're gone." She held up the cigar. "But Mr. Tudor left this."

"Show me anyway. I've never seen a spirit...except in the movies." Nick glanced at the cigar as they retraced her steps. "Weren't you scared?"

"Surprised but not scared. Seeing spirits felt good. Now I know there's more story beyond this."

An hour later, after finding no signs of Mr. Tudor or the dog, they were back at the stream filling the container.

"Do you believe me?" Katie asked.

"Of course."

After laying roses at Mr. Tudor's grave, Katie said, "We're gonna get their story told including what I saw today. I casually checked the Internet back in August for Mr. Tudor's name and nothing popped up. But I'll take another look. I could have missed something. And we'll have another talk with that apartment manager. Maybe some of Mr. Tudor's things are still around."

"The manager mentioned there was a collection of poems Mr. Tudor wrote…with the help of Sparky. It'd be cool if we find that document."

"Folks at Driscoll's will help, and we'll call the pastor at the retirement home." She rubbed Happy's back. "This little guy knows something." She glanced at the woods. "We'll come back next Wednesday evening with cigars, doggy biscuits…maybe a bottle of scotch. That's their special night. I'll bet they'll show up."

Nick smiled, and said, "That'll be a story worth telling."

Six Blocks Down

Jesse swiped his sweaty forehead. "Damn this heat. Let's head to Pappy's."

Charley leaned back on the metal bench. "That's six blocks down. The Raven's around the corner and cold booze is cold booze."

"Nope, it's gotta be Pappy's. Ain't been there in a while, but that's where I celebrated my twenty-first birthday fifty years ago today."

"Well happy birthday." Charley lit a cigarette and grabbed his cane. "Let's go."

Jesse Barnes lived alone in a rundown house near the railroad tracks on the outskirts of town. His wife Mary died of lung cancer years ago. Charley Wagner was seventy and shared a small apartment with his daughter and two grandkids.

Jesse pulled a wad of bills from his pocket. "I cashed my social security check. It feels good to have cash money. Even for a little while."

"Don't flash that around. You won't get bothered if they think you're broke."

"You can't count on that."

Charley nodded. "Yeah—you're right."

A speeding cab raced past as they hurried across the street.

"That guy almost hit me," Jesse said.

"I didn't know you could move that fast," Charley said.

"I can't—just got lucky. Think he would've stopped if I ended up sprawled on the sidewalk?"

"Not a chance in hell."

At the corner of Grand and Lexington, Jesse said, "Wait while I run into the drug store and get a pack of cigarettes. Anything you need?"

"Oh…a roll of gum will do."

A few minutes later, Jesse pushed open the glass door and lit a cigarette. A city bus pulled up as he tossed Charley his gum.

While the driver helped a couple of elderly women off, Charley said, "Let's take the bus. It's just fifty cents and we'll be at Pappy's in less than ten minutes."

Jesse glanced down Grand Avenue. "Let's walk."

They crossed Lexington and stopped in front of a burnt out shell of a single-story brick building. A red bike missing its rear wheel lay abandoned in a patch of weeds.

"Remember that old guy that lived here when we were kids? He'd sit out on a green lawn chair," Jesse said.

Charley nodded. "Yeah, he lived alone. A neighbor helped him to his chair same time every day. He'd tell neat stories about his time in the war. Now and then he'd give me a nickel to get a soda over at the drug store. Nice guy."

Jesse pointed. "He'd sit right about there, same spot all the time. There used to be a big oak shade tree around here. When I rode my bike past I wondered what it'd be like to be that guy." He gazed at the red bike. "It feels like five-minutes ago."

"Yesterdays pile up fast. Then one day you're just another broken-down old man."

"What was his name?"

"Akers…Frank Akers."

"Yeah, that's it. Let's see if he's buried over at Jefferson Barracks military cemetery. If he is, we'll pay our respects. I'll buy a dozen red roses."

"Why red roses?"

"Remember, he had that red rose bush near the house."

"Oh, yeah." Charley tapped his cane on the sidewalk. "I'll check it out tomorrow."

After crossing Franklin Avenue, they passed in front of a two-story brown brick building plastered with red and blue graffiti. Most windows were missing or broken.

As Jesse glanced up a couple of crows flew out of a second-story opening. He shook his head. "After they removed the bell and cross from the roof it looked like just another abandoned building." He turned to Charley. "I did my first communion and confirmation in there. At Christmas the nuns with help from men in the parish would set up a manger scene in the back of church surrounded by twenty-foot fir trees with soft, dark-green needles with those great smells. The trees were wrapped with special dark-blue lights. And remember that hill behind the church. When it snowed we'd race home after school and grab our sleds."

"I'd be there past dark and my mom would drag me home," Charley said.

"I was a repentant sinner back then. But since my wife died I haven't hung Christmas lights or put up a tree. I still get a few Christmas cards but don't send any."

"How long has Saint Michael's been closed?"

"Let's see…about twenty-five years ago for the church and the school ten years before that." Jesse slapped his hands together. "You know things are bad when God beats it out of town."

Two unshaven young men in undershirts and tattered jeans exited the building and asked for money. They left when Jesse and Charley turned them down.

"Homeless folks hang out in there now." Charley laughed, and said, "Think they're doing much praying between hits of whatever they're on?"

"Not from bums."

"My daughter and grandkids won't let me use the word 'bum' around the apartment. The accepted term is homeless."

"Banning a word don't convert bums into something they're not. That's like pretending two plus two equals five because I say so. Who's kidding who?"

A skinny woman with scraggly hair and yellowed teeth shouted down from the second floor. "You guys got money?"

After Jesse yelled "No," she tossed an empty wine bottle that shattered on the sidewalk.

"She's in her early thirties. I knew her dad," Charley said.

"She looks sixty. You wonder how people end up like that."

"She's drunk herself old."

Jesse kicked at the broken glass. "The bottom is getting crowded."

They crossed Chestnut Street and settled down on a bench in Fairgrounds Park.

Jesse pointed at the busted water fountain. "Why do that?"

"There don't need to be a reason."

"I played touch football here in high school. Now it's where people go to be bums together," Jesse said.

A cry drew their attention to a man poking a small dog with a stick.

Charley grabbed his cane. "I'm gonna break this over that bastard's head."

Before they got up, two men ran over, punched and kicked the bearded guy senseless, and rescued the animal.

"Ain't those the two characters we met a few minutes ago?" Jesse said.

"That's them."

Jesse waved them over, patted the dog, and handed each five dollars. After they left, he said, "Some bums surprise you."

Charley glanced down. "What the hell is that nasty lump?"

"Don't know." Jesse rubbed his ankle. "About six months ago it was the size of a marble and now its golf ball size."

"Does it hurt?"

"I slap an ice bag on it at night."

"What's the doctor say?"

"I ain't seen a doctor." Jesse flicked his cigarette. "It's part of getting old."

"I can give you the name of my doctor. He'd figure out what's going on. At least you'd know."

"I'll think about it."
"You want to take the bus the last couple of blocks?"
Jesse stretched his legs. "Nope, but let's rest a little."

Twenty minutes later they crossed Arsenal Street and strolled past the boarded up Olympia Theater.

Charley pointed his cane. "I went on my first date in there. I took Nancy Graff to see a Bogart film called *The Barefoot Contessa*."

"Nancy was a beautiful gal."

"Everybody said she looked just like Gene Tierney."

"Whatever happened to her?"

"She's up in New York. Doing OK—I hear."

"No surprise there. She always was a climber."

"Remember the popcorn and candy smells that hit you when you walked in? And they had air-conditioning before anyone else," Jesse said.

"That's right. On a Friday or Saturday night my mom and dad would go see a movie just to get out of the heat."

"Now people expect life to be air conditioned and it don't work that way."

Charley stepped around a candy bar covered in ants on the hot sidewalk. He noticed an ant dragging a fly covered in chocolate toward the grass.

Just past Tucker Boulevard a vacant lot was piled with plastic bags of trash, hot water heaters, rusty wash machines, and old auto parts. Clusters of gnats hovered patches of green slimy water.

Charley held his nose. "Whew, the smell of decay on a hot summer day."

"The gnats seem to be enjoying themselves," Jesse said.

"Don't let those crazy gnats fool you. I'll bet they're all scared to death. They know the west wind isn't coming."

At the roar of pop-pop and tires spinning, Charley said, "We didn't used to hear things like that."

A few seconds later a silver Mercedes packed with young men sped by.

Jesse pointed at a beauty supply store with metal bars on the windows and security buzzer for the front door. "I got my first job in there when it was a dime store. Used to clean up the storeroom, later worked the cash register." He laughed, and said, "We didn't sell wigs or hair shampoo."

Charley nodded. "The owner was named Joe."

Jesse scooped up a quarter on the sidewalk. "This bought a soda back in the day."

"With change left over." Charley said.

Two brown rats picked at a discarded sandwich on the sidewalk. A big black cat lunged from a nearby alley and caught one still gripping its food while the other escaped down a sewer.

They crossed Harper Street with Pappy's around the corner.

Jesse picked up the pace. "I hope old Bob is still bartending."

"Slow down," Charley said.

Jesse stared across the street. "Their parking lot is empty!"

"Shouldn't be this time of day."

They hurried past Casey's Tattoo Parlor and a boarded-up sandwich shop and faced the one-story wood-frame building that housed Pappy's. Grass and weeds rose from cracks in the parking lot and the faded black-walnut twin front doors were battered and padlocked.

Jesse rubbed the window and gazed inside. "It's empty."

Charley shaded his eyes as he walked under the torn canopy. "Everything gets dead and buried. It was Pappy's turn."

Jesse gripped the padlock and then looked across the street. "Let's ask those guys in front of the thrift store? They'd know about this."

"It is what it is. Leave it there." Charley lit a cigarette. "Let's get out of the sun. The bus heading back should arrive in ten minutes."

Inside the bus shelter a skinny gray-haired woman in a short-sleeve white blouse and blue skirt mumbled as she held a small book.

She glanced over as Jesse sat down. "Prayers get me through the day."

"Yes, ma'am," Jesse responded.

She shoved the book inside her purse and smiled through several missing front teeth. "I'm Agnes Hoffman."

"I'm Jesse Barnes and he's Charley Wagner."

A moment later Agnes scooped up a rock and flung it at a couple of pigeons poking around in the grass. "Nasty creatures covered with lice always looking for a handout. They're horrible."

Jesse shrugged and flicked his cigarette to the sidewalk. "Here comes our ride."

An orange bus covered with red graffiti pulled up. Jesse helped Agnes onto the seat behind the driver and sat across from her.

Bursts of laughter followed by silence and laughter again drew their attention to the back of the bus. In the last seat an unshaven man in T-shirt, cut-off jeans, and sandals sat shaking and laughing.

"Oh, that guy," Agnes commented. "He's on something."

She noticed Charley chewing. "Got any more gum?"

"Take what's left," Charley said.

"Wild cherry!"

Agnes gripped her seat when the bus bounced in and out of a wide, deep pothole.

She turned to Jesse. "That damn hole has been there over a year and getting bigger all the time."

At the Franklin stop, Charley said, "We'll walk you home."

"Thanks," Agnes said.

The bus belched a cloud of dark exhaust as it pulled away.

Franklin Avenue was a wide street of Victorian-style homes built in the late nineteenth century for wealthy manufacturers, retailers, and beer barons.

Agnes made a fist as they walked down the block. "Half these homes are occupied by panhandlers, dope addicts, and street thugs. Derelicts expecting something for nothing."

"If we're banning words 'free' ought to be included," Charley said.

"I'll stamp an amen to that," she said.

They passed under a forty-foot tall maple tree wracked with dead branches.

"This street had the best shade," Agnes said.

Sirens wailed in the distance as they headed up the cracked sidewalk splattered with glass and heaved up in spots by tree roots.

"I'm up here on the right," Agnes said. "I rent out a couple of rooms and have to share the bathroom and kitchen with a young gal with a boyfriend who beats her. She's twenty-five and gets more money from the government than I get on social security."

She raised her voice. "I pray for her, but God expects people to step up."

"That's old-God thinking. He's left town," Jesse said.

Agnes settled down on a green lawn chair in front of her home. "I can make iced tea and throw some chicken pot pies in the oven." She pointed at a couple of chairs leaning against the side of the house. "We can eat and talk out here."

"Got any beef pot pies?" Charley asked.

Jesse tapped Charley on the shoulder. "We gotta get going."

Charley glanced at Agnes. "I forgot we're heading to the Raven."

"Last night the bartender told me the Raven's owner blew his brains out a couple of days ago and they're gonna close next week. I don't know where I'm gonna do my drinking," Agnes said.

"Didn't see that on the news," Jesse said.

"Fred was just another nobody as far as they're concerned," she said.

They said their goodbyes and headed up the street, when Agnes shouted, "I'll pick up beef pot pies for next time."

Jesse waved, and said, "You think she's right?"

"About Fred? Yep."

"Hell, he just bought the place a couple years ago. I wonder what happened."

"I don't try to figure stuff out anymore. There's one less good man in the world and the reason is between him and his Maker."

"We're running out of things to do around here."

Charley laughed, and said, "Well…there's always pot pies with Agnes."

From the corner of Grand and Lexington, third building on the right, stood a small wooden structure. Its roof covered with broken and split brown asphalt tiles. Above the narrow entrance a metallic Raven attached to a short metal rod greeted visitors. Other than a laundry directly across the street, the other retail locations were boarded up.

Charley held the door. "Let's spend the afternoon here and then head over to my place for dinner. My daughter is cooking a roast and we'll celebrate your birthday. Later we'll put a bag of ice on your ankle and watch my favorite Bogart film *Dead Reckoning*. It's on the late show."

"Thanks, Charley, that's damn decent of you."

What about Bonnie?

Steve shoved his phone in his shirt pocket, and faced his buddies. "The boss wants us on the Proctor job by eight sharp."

Harry shook his head. "That's way on the other side of town."

Dave tossed the tool boxes in the back of the dusty red pickup truck. "We better hurry."

Steve pulled out of the parking lot and swung left. "We'll take Hwy. 70, it'll save five minutes."

"I don't know. It's always packed, particularly Monday mornings." Dave said.

Harry rolled down the window, and lit a cigarette.

Dave flipped on the radio while Steve sped up and passed a couple of slow-moving cars.

Around seven-forty five, they were driving through a wooded region, when Harry slapped the dashboard. "Pull over and stop."

Steve parked on the side of the road. "What the hell is the problem? We only got fifteen minutes to get to the job site."

Harry got out and walked back toward a small black figure lying on the side of the busy road. A few seconds later, Dave caught up with him. Steve watched for a moment, and then followed the other two.

Harry was holding the figure, when Dave remarked, "It's only a dead cat."

Harry examined the tag around the animal's neck. "Her name was Bonnie. I'll call the number on the tag and let her owners know, they must be frantic." He set the animal down in the grass, and then stepped toward the woods to get away from the noisy traffic.

Steve and Dave watched Harry pace back and forth and begin shouting.

Harry walked up shaking his head. "I talked to some lady, and then a guy. I told them where they could come get their cat, and the jerks didn't seem to care. How do you like that shit!"

Steve shrugged. "I guess we go."

"Not yet." Harry gestured toward an oak tree about seventy feet from the road. "There's nice grass and good shade under that tree. We'll bury her there."

Dave ran toward the truck. "I'll grab the shovels."

"The boss ain't going to like this," Steve said.

"This is more important than being a few minutes late for work." Harry said. "If you don't think he'll understand, then make up some shit."

Steve called the boss and said traffic was backed up and they'd be a little delayed.

Harry cradled Bonnie's still soft and warm body as he walked over to the oak tree. The crackling flow of a nearby creek could be heard rounding its way through the woods. To the right of the oak a small stand of blossoming cherry trees shared a warm sweet scent pushed by a light breeze.

With his sleeves rolled up, Dave approached with a shovel in one hand and a large metal tool box in the other. "I emptied this out, I think she'll fit."

Harry brushed her eyes close, removed a few specks of gravel from her fur, and then placed her in the tool box.

Dave finished digging, and then reached for the metal box.

Harry held out his hand. "I want to give her something to take on her journey." He retrieved from his pants pocket a black rosary, kissed the crucifix, and laid the rosary next to the cat. Then he closed the metal box.

Dave placed the box in the hole, Harry scattered a handful of earth on the box, and then Dave refilled the hole.

After tamping the last of the dirt down with his hands, Dave stared at Harry. "Do you want to say a few words?"

Harry glanced at the morning traffic shuttling by, and then up at the cloudless sky. "Yes, I do." He removed his cap, while Dave rolled down his sleeves and dusted off his jeans.

Standing over the small mound of dirt, Harry made the sign of the cross, and bowed. "Lord, we commend the departing soul of Your good servant—Bonnie. She had a short, tough life, yet I'm sure there were rich moments. Her work is done here, and we know she's been delivered to a better place. I think she'll enjoy spending time relaxing in the woods, resting in the shade of an oak tree. You know, cats like their sleep." He dropped to one knee. "Lord, one more thing. Please introduce Bonnie to another recent arrival, my brother Greg. He loved cats, and he and Bonnie will be happy together."

Harry pointed at a white stone a few feet away. "Let's use that to mark her grave."

Steve and Dave struggled with the heavy stone, but finally placed it on the small mound of dirt.

When they reached the truck, Harry noticed a rabbit and two gray squirrels near the grave. Gathered above them on a low hanging branch of the oak tree, a trio of whippoorwills had begun to twitter and sing.

Steve started up the engine. "Harry, I've seen hundreds of animals in distress or dead. I'm always going to remember this one."

"Death is inevitable, but it doesn't have to be alone, abandoned, and on the side of some damn road. How many so-called nice people drove past her in their cars and trucks? We should be better than that."

As they pulled away, Dave said, "Let's come back in a month and lay flowers on her grave."

Steve nodded agreement.

"You bet," Harry said.

Shadows in the Maelstrom

On a hot July morning in St. Louis, Gus Davenport, a young police sergeant, drove a rusty gray van down a narrow side street littered with black trash bags and broken glass. Across from him sat Blake, a feared state security detective known for his explosive temper and violent history.

The van rolled to a stop in front of a brown-brick building with a glass storefront. A sign in the window read *Bureau of Interrogation*. Gus opened the rear of the sweltering van while Blake stood with his hand next to his holstered firearm. Dave, old and slow, his face dripping in sweat, exited the van. Jack dropped a cigarette butt as he jumped out. He was followed by Steve, a skinny twelve-year-old.

"I got their cellphones in the van."

Blake nodded at Gus and then tripped Steve as he walked past. "Stay on your feet, kid."

Steve muttered "Jerk" as he bounced to his feet.

Blake opened the Bureau's glass front door and they were greeted by a damp, musty smell as they passed through a small vestibule. He ordered the prisoners onto a green leather couch, and then banged on a door that read Private, and shouted, "They're here."

Doris, a slim, dark-haired woman, opened the door and glanced at the couch. "That one fella is so young. Can I get him a soda?"

"Nope."

"The boss is making an arrest that'll be on the news. I expect him and the rest of the guys to be back in about an hour." She closed the door as Blake sat in a large easy chair facing the couch. Gus stood next to the door. The clock on the wall showed nine-fifteen.

The waiting room's floor was light-gray concrete; its blue plaster walls had several large cracks and breaks along the base. A small chandelier hung in the middle of the room. Beyond the door marked Private were four interrogation rooms and the boss' office.

Blake lit a cigar and grinned at the prisoners. "Don't make trouble."

The older man, Dave, glanced over at Steve. "How'd a kid like you get here?"

Steve brushed back his curly blond hair. "I must've said something at school. When they grabbed me up this morning they said a teacher turned me in."

"Talking too much is dangerous."

"I'll be more careful in the future."

Blake blew a smoke ring, and said, "What future."

"What'd your parents say?" Dave asked.

"I barely remember my parents. They died when I was three. I've been living at a state home. When the police showed up the woman running the place took them to my room, and then she ran and hid in the bathroom."

Dave turned to Jack. "What'd you do to get here?"

Jack shrugged. "I don't know. I hope it ain't too serious."

When Jack began to light a cigarette, Blake shouted, "Who said you could smoke?"

He stared at the detective's smoldering cigar as he put the cigarette back in the pack.

Blake leaned back in the easy chair, took a puff, and said, "You got a problem?"

"Nope."

Blake pointed at the clock on the wall. "We got fifty minutes. That's when the fun starts. The boss man is a helluva problem solver."

Steve looked at Dave. "What'd an old guy like you do?"

"The state says I have silver coins hidden somewhere."

"Where'd they get that idea?"

"From the neighborhood snitch, a nasty young gal named Peggy. She makes money off that program that pays a ten percent finder's fee for helping the government uncover private hidden assets. She's turned in half the neighborhood on spec. They hauled me out of bed this morning and right now are tearing my house apart. Tomorrow they're bringing a backhoe to tear up the yard. They ain't going to find anything."

"What happens then?"

"That's why I'm here. This is where they yank their truth out of you."

"Our truth is the only truth that counts," Blake said, laughing. "Old man, I'm gonna enjoy watching them work on you."

"What about your wife?" Steve asked.

"She died before things got bad. Thank God she didn't experience this."

"You're old enough to remember a different world. How'd all this happen?"

"Kid, it came at us a little at a time—always claiming to defend freedom and democracy by reducing it. Some folks made noise, sounded warnings, tried to stop it. I should've done more to fight this. Maybe we deserve it for being careless with truth and our freedoms."

"Would've, could've, should've is loser talk." Blake tapped the ash off his cigar. "Folks need to stop looking back and calling it the good old days. We wouldn't be here if those days were that damned good."

Blake pointed at Jack. "Share your story—fat boy. Tell them what you did." He set the cigar in the ashtray. "He turned in his brother and uncle to save his ass. He even asked for a reward."

"Since he helped you catch them…why's he here?" Steve asked.

"Anybody that turns in his brother for money is a rat. We use them, but we never trust rats." He leaned toward Dave. "Did you and the kid tell him anything on the ride over? If you did he'll tell the boss all about it."

Jack shook his head in denial.

A scratching sound drew Steve's attention to a small break in the plaster a couple inches above the floor. A tiny head popped out and stared at him.

Steve pointed, and said, "Looks like we got a friend." He smiled at the mouse and signaled with his hands for it to come over.

The thin light-gray creature sped across the floor, stopping at Steve's right shoe, and then jumped into his cupped hands.

"I'm gonna call him Larry," Steve declared.

The mouse flapped its tail as Dave and Jack smiled.

Blake jumped out of his chair and smacked the mouse from Steve's hands. "Just sit there and be fucking quiet."

The mouse ran under the couch and then headed back toward the wall. Blake blocked its path and chased it around the room stomping and laughing. When the mouse appeared cornered, Steve ran over and shoved Blake. At that moment the mouse darted back inside the crack in the wall.

"The mouse didn't do anything wrong!" Steve shouted. "Why kill him?"

Screaming profanities, Blake drew his gun and aimed it at Steve.

A shot rang out, followed by another. Blake stammered and then dropped to the floor, his face covered in blood.

Doris opened the door. "What the hell is going on?" She stared at Blake's body and then at Gus as he holstered his gun. "Did you do that?"

"Blake was gonna kill the kid. I couldn't let that happen."

"Is he dead?"

"Yep, I'm sure."

She glanced at the blood pooling around Blake's body, and then checked the clock on the wall. "God help us when the boss walks in on this bloody mess."

"We need to get out of here…now!" Gus yelled.

Dave and Jack headed toward the door, while Doris shouted. "I'm going with you guys."

Gus grabbed Steve's hand. "Come on, kid."

At the door, Steve said, "What about Larry?"

The mouse jumped out of the crack in the wall, scrambled around Blake's body, and followed everyone out the door.

The van sped up the street and turned left. Doris sat in the front. In the back were Steve, Dave, and Jack, and Larry poking his head from Steve's shirt pocket.

Doris checked her watch. "They should be back in about twenty minutes. Figure another ten or fifteen minutes while they sort things out. That's about all the time we got before they start coming after us."

Gus glanced at Doris. "Yeah, and we gotta ditch this van and grab another vehicle."

"You mean jack a car or truck?" Steve shouted. "That'll just get us in worse trouble."

Doris swung around and faced the men in the back. "Blake is dead back there. It's a bullet for everyone…if they catch us."

"You can always give evidence and claim you were kidnapped," Dave said.

"Yeah, you got no worries," Jack said.

"I ain't going back." She opened her large purse and held up a .38 caliber handgun. "This is a one-way trip for me."

Gus grabbed the gun. "I'll take that."

"Damn, I was hoping to go to college," Steve said.

"That dream died when you got arrested," Gus said.

Gus turned up an alley and pulled over. "We're about to meet people devoted to bringing sanity and a sense of justice to our world. Are you guys in or not? If not, I'll drop you somewhere and you'll be on your own. What's it gonna be?"

"I'm in," Jack said.

"Me, too," Dave said. "I've still got enough energy to help."

They drove a few blocks and arrived at an empty gravel-covered parking lot and stopped in front of an old warehouse with a rusty sign that read HARPERS on the front. Gus honked the horn and the large twin metal doors were pulled open by several men. Once inside this twenty-five-thousand-square-foot space a guy named Jeb, in jeans, wearing a tan cowboy hat approached the driver's side door while six armed men stood near the van.

"What happened, Gus?" Jeb asked.

"I shot and killed Blake. That nut was running around the interrogation office like a mad dog." Gus pointed inside the van. "Blake pulled a gun after that spunky kid stood up to him. He would've shot the kid right there in the office waiting room. I didn't have any choice."

"I guess the folks inside the van are witnesses?"

"Yep."

"Where's the body?"

"It's where it dropped. We had to get out of there in a hurry."

"Who are these folks?"

"The guys are all up on charges…including the kid. The woman is the office administrator."

"She works for the state!"

"After the shooting she said she wanted to come with us." Gus shrugged, and said, "What could I do?"

Jeb grabbed Gus' arm. "Can we trust them?"

"They seem OK, but who knows?"

"Where'd the kid come from?"

"The bums hauled him in because he said something at school they didn't like."

"What about his parents?"

"Both are dead. We're gonna have to take care of him until we figure something out."

"How about taking him and the others to Mom's?" Gus said.

"That'll work out great. She just got word to me she's looking for a new group. I'll let her know to expect you guys."

"It's been a couple of years since I've heard that raspy voice of hers."

"It's all those cigarettes she smokes." Jeb shook his head. "I was there six months ago and she looked tired and pale."

Gus nodded, and said, "I wish she'd quit those cigarettes."

"She'll quit if she wants to not because anyone tells her to."

"I've never heard her complain about anything. What a tough old bird."

Jeb leaned against the van. "Too bad you lost your cover over this. But, you did what you had to do."

"I'm glad it fell to me," Gus said. "That monster needed killing."

"Blake was one of their heroes, so they'll be coming after you with everything they got. Watch the phone traffic."

"I took their phones when they got arrested."

Jeb pointed at two trucks with green canvases hung over the passenger section parked in the back next to three large black Jeeps. "They'll be looking for your van, so drive one of these up to Mom's. Do you have a preference?"

"We'll take a Jeep."

"Good, they're gassed up, so you won't have to stop for fuel."

Jeb led Gus to a rack of clothes near the restroom door. "You need to get out of that uniform. Find a work shirt and jeans that fit."

Gus smiled, and said, "By the way, have you got cheese around here?"

"You want a cheese sandwich?"

"Nope, just a slice for that kid's friend, Larry."

"Who the hell is Larry?"

"A gritty mouse that joined us back there. It came out of nowhere and one thing led to another...crazy."

Jeb laughed, and said, "You never know, do you." As he walked toward the refrigerator, he said, "You guys, including Larry, need to hurry before they seal off this area."

Doris held her nose and complained about the awful oil and gas smells as she climbed into the front of the Jeep. Larry was back in Steve's shirt pocket. He had stopped eating his cheese after he spotted a dead mouse crushed in a trap next to the work bench.

Fifteen minutes later, Gus drove the Jeep onto Grand Avenue, and then took the exit to Hwy. 70. From there it was a three-hour drive to Mom's place buried deep in the wooded hills of the Missouri Ozarks.

An hour into the drive all the radio stations were reporting the story of Blake's murder and to be on the lookout for the gang responsible…including Doris. A one hundred-thousand- dollar reward was posted.

Doris flipped off the radio. "That's enough."

"They didn't say suspects, they said perpetrators," Steve said. He rolled down the window. "Ain't we gonna get a trial?"

Gus passed a car, and said, "If they catch us, we'll get to sign a confession before we get executed. A confession proves they're right, and they're always right. Welcome to our justice system."

"That's the lay of the land, kid," Jack said.

At this point, Gus had everyone slip on a mask covering their eyes to prevent them from seeing the roads he was taking.

With ten miles to go Gus allowed them to remove the masks as the Jeep drove through a twisted green thicket of forest strewn with fallen tree branches, large potholes, and overgrown shrubs brushing the Jeep as it drove past.

Doris rolled down the window. "My goodness, how do you navigate through this jungle?"

"You don't unless you know the way," Gus said.

"I haven't seen any street signs?"

"The roads we built never had any. We tore down all the others."

He swung the Jeep onto a dirt road with a large oak tree on each side of the entrance. "You can't see it from here, but Mom's place is a mile ahead. When it rains heavy or there's a big snow you have to park and walk from here."

Gus and Jack dragged away a large tree limb blocking the path while Doris carried a turtle that was in front of the Jeep and set it under a red mulberry tree.

Five minutes later, Gus pointed. "That's where we'll stay for now."

Perched on a grassy hilltop was a two-story log cabin with a large front porch and a gray-stone fireplace at one end.

They parked near a stand of sugar maple trees and followed a gravel path lined on both sides with radiant red, yellow and pink roses flooding the surrounding air with their sweet welcoming scent.

As they approached the cabin, a thin woman with a big smile and shoulder-length gray hair walked out on the porch and waved.

Gus ran up and gave her a hug. "Hello, Mom, you look good. These folks are friends of ours and need your help."

"That's what I'm here for." She slung her arm around Steve's waist. "I hear you're a brave young man…confronting that evil Blake the way you did."

As they reached the door, the mouse stared at Mom from Steve's shirt pocket.

She smiled, and said, "Who's that?"

"That's Larry," Steve said.

"Welcome, Larry. Thanks for joining us."

Mom led them to a room with several bookshelves, three large black-leather couches, and an easy chair next to the floor-to-ceiling fireplace.

She lit a cigarette, and said, "The state wants you guys real bad. Blake was one of their favorite monsters."

"I shot him," Gus said.

"You'll all go down for it—if they catch you." She took a deep drag, and said, "We ain't gonna let that happen."

"My friends will wonder where I'm at," Steve said.

"We're your friends," she said. "We got enough food to last for months." She flicked an ash off the cigarette. "You'll love this place. I've got books, and there's a lake you can fish and swim."

She stood next to the window and pointed. "You guys need to walk the woods at first light or dusk and experience soothing sights like moonlight shimmering off the lake, sounds of birds calling to each other, and all the sweet smells that nature provides. You learn so much out there."

"Fishing sounds good," Dave said.

"I'll show you the best spots to toss a line," she said.

"I love hiking trails," Doris said.

"Don't expect well-worn paths," Mom said. "I'll get you a pair of boots."

Mom tossed her cigarette into the fireplace. "Let's head to the kitchen, you guys look hungry."

The kitchen had a wooden table that seated ten. Fresh water was pumped in from a well, and a gas generator supplied energy for a stove, a refrigerator, and a large freezer. The floors throughout the cabin were solid oak. The kitchen door opened to a big deck overlooking a vast wooded area with a sparkling lake just a few hundred feet from the cabin.

Mom opened the refrigerator and brought out a plate of carved ham, slices of cheese, and a loaf of bread. "It ain't the Ritz, but you won't starve while you're here. There's a plastic container of mustard on the countertop."

She set a large jug of tea on the table. "I've got a hot cherry pie for dessert."

She looked at Larry. "I didn't forget about you." She set a plate on the floor with a piece of cheese and a smear of peanut butter.

Larry jumped down and went straight for the cheese.

Doris took a drink, and said, "I didn't see any other vehicles when we rolled up. How do you get supplied with food and other stuff?"

"I don't drive," Mom said. "In fact, I haven't left these woods in over thirty years. There's nothing out there I want." She leaned back in the chair. "Two of our people stop by three or four times a week to bring supplies and do minor odd jobs." She laughed, and said, "They also check to make sure I didn't fall and break my neck."

"You're isolated. It might take 911 a week to find you up here," Doris said.

"Everyone dies…sooner or later. There's no point worrying about it."

Ten minutes later, Mom rose and pointed to a stack of paper on the countertop. "There's a form you guys need to fill out. It covers background stuff, and gets your height/weight, shoe size, etc. You're gonna need a change of clothes while you're here. We'll also create your new IDs."

Steve set his sandwich down. "Why?"

"You need to disappear for a long time. They're waiting and watching for you to contact family or friends."

"I'll be careful."

"You're not going back." She put her hand on Steve's shoulder. "If you reach out to any of your friends they'll catch you and people will suffer as a result. You know about Harper and me, and they have their ways of getting that from you. You can't negotiate, make deals, or expect anything resembling justice from them folks."

"That's the word, kid," Gus said. "Whatever they do is called legal. But it's corrupt to the core."

"Get those forms filled out," Mom said. She then walked out to the deck and lit a cigarette.

Around six o'clock the next morning, a noise woke Steve. He jumped out of bed and pulled back the curtains. A late model black SUV had parked near the front porch and the woman he knew as Mom was talking to the driver.

Steve hurried to the other bed and shook Gus till he woke. "Hey, your mom is talking to some dude out there."

Gus sat up, and said, "So what, she's a busy lady." He reached down for his shoes. "And, she's not my mom. Everybody just calls her Mom."

"What's her real name?"

"I don't know. I've never met anyone who knows. It doesn't matter."

"Ok…Ok."

Steve watched the woman hand the driver a package, and wave as the vehicle drove down the hill.

Thirty minutes later, Mom rapped on the bedroom door. "It's time for breakfast! Larry and I have been up for an hour."

Steve walked into the kitchen, and Mom said, "We've been waiting. Take a seat."

There was a large platter at the center of the table piled high with warm fluffy pancakes. Next to it were two large silver serving containers filled with maple syrup, and a large pitcher of tea.

Mom held up her hand. "We give thanks before we eat." She recited a brief prayer, and turned to Steve. "You're way too skinny. Take a big stack and soak them in that maple syrup."

While Steve slid pancakes on his plate, Gus said, "Leave a few for us, kid."

"Larry didn't want pancakes," Mom said. "He's outside feasting on what nature provides."

"It won't taste as good as your pancakes," Jack said.

Gus nodded. "Amen to that."

"Nature helped," she said. "That syrup is from the maple trees out there."

After breakfast, Mom gathered everyone out on the deck. "We're working on your new identities and where to best place you. We got a big network, so it shouldn't take long." She lit a cigarette, and said, "Your extra clothes should be here in a few days. Not suits and ties, but working class shirts, jeans, and shoes."

She gazed at the lake. "Who wants to go fishing?"

"I do," Jack said.

"I'll get the gear and show you the best spots to fish." She pointed, and said, "You too, Steve."

"I've never fished," Steve said.

"It's time you learned."

Three hours later, they arrived back with stringers loaded with catfish and largemouth bass.

"Wow," Gus yelled as they approached the deck.

Jack raised one of the stringers. "I've never seen anything like it."

Mom touched Steve's shoulder. "This young man turned out to be quite the fisherman. Tonight we're gonna have a hell-of-a fish fry after he learns how to clean them."

That evening, after Gus lit the logs in the fireplace, Mom invited everyone to sit while she opened two bottles of sweet-red wine.

After filling everyone's glass, including Steve's, she scooted her large green chair near the fireplace. "The bounty for you guys is up to two-hundred thousand for Blake's death. In a week it'll be a half million. But, don't worry; just a handful of people know you're here and they can't be bought."

She pointed at Doris. "Why'd you run? You weren't in any trouble back there."

"I couldn't take the screams, the blood, and the horrors anymore. I wanted to get out and this came up. Blake was the worst of the bunch." She took a drink, and said, "I heard the pop-pop, opened the door, and saw Blake lying there with Gus holding a gun. I ran because I was scared and knew it was time to break from all of that."

"What'd you do there?" Mom asked.

"Answered the phone, kept track of appointments, just general office duties. But as long as I stayed I was part of it."

"I understand you wanted out. But, will you help us…the resistance?"

Doris nodded, and said, "I'll do anything to fight this evil system."

"Ok, I'll see you get placed. There's something up in New York City where you'd be a good fit."

Larry caught everyone's attention when he scampered across the floor and disappeared in the corner.

Mom smiled, and said, "I wondered where he got to."

"What have you got planned for me?" Gus asked.

"I hope you don't mind the cold. You're heading to a small farm town in northern Minnesota. That'll be your base of operations."

"To do what?"

"Identify and screen folks from small communities ready to help us. It'll be a change of pace, but you're skill sets will be a good fit there."

She refilled Dave's glass, and said, "You walk with a limp. I'll get you a cane. Is there anything serious going on there?"

Dave shook his head. "It's just old-age arthritis. I've been living with it for years."

"I'll make sure you get sent someplace warm, maybe Florida or California. It'll be easier on your old bones." She took a drink, and said, "I read you're a retired accountant."

"A CPA," Dave insisted.

"We can use people who understand finance and budgets." She pointed at Jack. "Your form was fuzzy about why you got arrested. Fill me in."

Jack finished his drink, and reached for a cigarette. "Do you mind if I smoke?"

"Go ahead."

After several drags, he said, "I don't know why they arrested me. No specific charge was shown on the arrest warrant. Blake told these guys I ratted on my brother, which was a lie." He took another puff, and shrugged. "I don't know why I got picked up."

"About your brother, we know you didn't turn him in." She looked at the others. "His brother was part of the resistance and got caught due to carelessness from a member of his team. Those things happen."

Steve raised his hand. "Why did they say he ratted on his brother?"

Mom leaned back in her chair. "Publicizing stories like that says somebody is always watching and willing to turn you in…even family. Totalitarian systems survive on fear and terror." She smiled, and said, "And you don't have to raise your hand to get permission to speak or ask questions around here."

She glanced over at Jack, and said, "We'll find a place for you."

She faced Steve. "What would you like to do?"

He shrugged. "I don't know."

"What classes did you like at school?"

"I liked learning about ancient Greeks and Romans."

"That's great. What else?"

"I loved reading poetry."

"Poetry!" she said. "That's what this evening needs."

She retrieved two books from the bookshelf, put them next to her chair, and then headed toward the kitchen. At the door, she turned, and said, "Gus, throw more logs on the fire while I get another bottle of wine."

Five minutes later, she set the bottle on the coffee table and glanced at the fire as it crackled and blazed. "There's nothing better than fine wine with great poetry and friends. Poetry takes you any place your mind is willing to go. We'll start with Shelley's *Ode to the West Wind* and then Keats great ode *To Autumn.*"

She smiled as she read, stopping at the end of each stanza to glance at the others. When finished, she said, "Take time to think about the wisdom of those poems. You'll be richer for it…and no state can take that away."

She had spent an hour lecturing and answering questions about poets and poetry, when Steve asked, "Who's your favorite poet?"

"That's easy, John Keats." She leaned toward Steve. "His poetry is still relevant two hundred years after his death. He lived a short, challenged life, but his wisdom is eternal." She handed Steve one of the books. "Get to know him. It'll be worth your while."

Twenty minutes later, with the fire dying out, Mom rose, and said, "Tomorrow we start our project."

"What kind of project?" Jack asked.

"I'll fill you in after breakfast." She glanced at the windowsill and winked. "You too, Larry."

The next morning, Mom gathered everyone out on the deck, and said, "I want you to leave something here for me to remember you. Depending on time of the year, it could be helping me plant a garden, cut down a tree, chop firewood. If you're handy, maybe it's repairing something."

She gripped the bannister. "About ten years ago a guy named Danny found a dead fox. He buried it while I cried reading words over it." She pointed at the woods. "I know where it's buried, and where Danny is today."

"What have you got in mind for us?" Jack asked.

"We're gonna widen the path that leads to that fishing spot you went to yesterday. Then we'll place a park-type bench under that oak tree. The bench and tools are in the shed." As she descended the stairs, she said, "The six of us will have this done in a few hours."

"Seven, counting Larry," Steve said.

"Of course…seven."

Two hours later, Jack and Gus placed the bench in a shaded area about twenty feet from the lake. Mom sat and watched a bluebird poke the ground for a meal while the others gathered around her.

Jack dropped his rake, and said, "Next year that path will be overgrown."

"Somebody will clear it again," she said. "This bench, the shade, and those fish will be waiting for them." She clasped her hands. "Tomorrow we'll pack a lunch and picnic out here. And we'll read poetry. It'll be Byron."

"You sure like poetry," Doris said.

Mom smiled, and said, "I taught a course on the Romantics at a big eastern university, and had several books published. I was quite the rising star."

"Wow, I never knew that," Gus said.

"That's a lifetime ago. But, you never lose your love for poetry."

The next week, Gus left for Minnesota, two weeks after that Doris headed to New York to work and make contacts in the theatre district. At the end of September, Dave and Jack arrived in San Francisco to operate a coffee shop which served as a front for the resistance.

Mom stared at the calendar hanging on the kitchen wall, and muttered, "Another year down the drain."

"What was that?" Steve said.

"It's already October…eat your breakfast." She glanced over. "It looks like rain. We'll spend the day inside, build a fire, read poetry, and discuss the lives of Wordsworth and Coleridge."

She sat, and said, "One of these days I'm giving you a test to see how much you've learned."

"I'm ready."

"We'll see. By the way, tomorrow a guy's stopping by to measure you for a suit."

"Why do I need a suit?"

"Every young man should have one for special occasions. I've picked a dark-blue material with pinstripes. Before you leave, I'll get a photo of you wearing it."

"When do I leave?"

"I'm making sure you land well and have a good future. But there's no hurry."

Three weeks later, on the fireplace mantle was a framed photo of Steve in his new suit with Mom standing next to him.

They fished, planted roses and a dozen scotch pines, canned fruit, baked sweet cherry pies and chocolate cakes from scratch, rescued an injured rabbit, and circled the lake strolling past fields of fast-fading colors while discussing the world and how to meet its challenges. Weather permitting, Sunday mornings they picnicked at the lake. Most evenings were spent reading poetry and other great works of literature.

In early December, Mom retrieved a ring from her pocket and placed it on Steve's finger. "It belonged to someone very dear to me." She gave him a hug. "Wear it always."

"I will. Who'd it belong to?"

"I'll tell you…someday."

She poured herself and Steve a mug of hot chocolate, and said, "Tonight we'll discuss Aristotle's views on ethics, good citizenship, and education."

"No poetry?" Steve asked.

From her easy chair she watched the flames dance in the fireplace. "Philosophers and poets are brothers that touch all we know, want to know, or can know. They'll help you discover truth, and truth sets everything in motion. You can't arrive at good without it. Never forget that."

"I won't."

A couple days later, Steve opened a drawer while searching for a book, and found a loaded revolver. He held it for a few seconds and put it back. He never mentioned his discovery to Mom.

On a crisp Sunday night, a week before Christmas, Mom was out on the deck identifying the constellations as Steve stared at the starlit sky.

She paused, and said, "Night is a perfect time to think, to question, to dream, to discover your voice and where it fits." She placed her hand on his shoulder. "You're going to help rescue us from this dark place someday."

"Will I be as important as you?"

"I don't do anything special. Helping people escape and resist tyranny is everybody's job." She leaned against the bannister. "Maybe I'm just an old lady dreaming. But, I believe the world will know and listen to your voice."

Suddenly a shooting star blazed across the night sky.

After it disappeared, she said, "It's getting cold. Let's go in."

Early the next morning, she shook Steve awake, and said, "Hurry up and get dressed. It's time for you to go."

"Go where?" Steve looked at the clock. "It's five o'clock."

"I've packed your clothes and put a thermos of hot tea and a couple of sandwiches in a bag." She tossed his winter coat on the chair. "Put your boots on. It's been snowing for an hour." She turned at the door. "Hurry, the Jeep is waiting."

He threw off the covers. "What's happened?"

"You're moving."

"Why now?"

"I'll be outside. We'll talk there."

Ten minutes later, Steve walked out on the porch. The Jeep's engine idled as its busy wipers brushed away falling snow. The grass was buried in snow. Mom stood next to the Jeep in her blue overcoat, white boots, with a bright red scarf covering her gray hair.

As she approached, Steve pointed at a nearby hill. "You promised we'd go sledding at the first snow, and put up a Christmas tree this week."

"I know…I know." She shrugged, and said, "We don't always get what we want."

"Why do I have to leave now?"

"Last night government security people raided our Harper warehouse. That's where you and your companions stopped before coming here. The shootout left a number of people dead. Anyone that survived will be in government hands. One guy there knows about this place. I trust him, but they have their ways of extracting information. At this point we just don't know."

As the wind picked up, Steve glanced at the snow-packed hill. "Maybe that guy didn't survive. Anyway, I'm sure he wouldn't talk."

"I won't take a chance with your safety. You'll be staying with a nice couple in rural Idaho. You'll get there sometime tomorrow. They're good people. You'll be fine."

"Are you coming with me?"

"This is my home. I'm not leaving."

"What if they come and try and grab you?"

She glanced at the cabin. "It doesn't matter. I'm not leaving."

Movement drew their attention near the door. It was Larry sitting atop a pile of fresh-cut logs.

"Larry's staying. He'll be ok," she said.

She gave Steve a hug, and said, "Always be a voice for truth."

"I will."

After Steve got in the Jeep, she signaled for him to roll down the window. "I packed a couple of books I want you to read."

He wiped away a tear. "When can I come back?"

"I don't know." She turned and headed to the porch. "I wish I knew."

He watched her wave from the porch as the Jeep moved down the hill. After the cabin disappeared from sight he prayed for her safety and vowed she would be proud of him.

Don't Pass the Exits

Don't Pass the Exits

About the Author

Hourston's other works of fiction include:

Monsters on Trial
What happens when America grants its mad, bad monsters legal rights? The answer is found in nine exciting short stories where Mike Hoffmann and his team battle vampires, werewolves, zombies, and other goblins—mostly in court. This book is available at Amazon in paperback and e-Book. It's also available at Barnes and Noble, and Kobo as an e-Book.

Tales of the Deep State
Travel from New York, to Washington, to California, to Utopia, Tennessee, and small town Missouri and learn who's really in charge out there and how they get and keep their hold on power. Meet the bad guys and the Americans that stand up to them. This book is available in paperback and e-Book at Amazon. It's also available at Barnes and Noble, and Kobo as an e-Book.

R.I.P. When All is Said and Done
Stories that chase the meaning of justice and revenge, encounter the afterlife, reflect on times gone by, and close with a young poet in search of a poem. This book is available in paperback and e-Book at Amazon.

Hourston has master degrees in history (MA) and business administration (MBA) from the University of Missouri-St. Louis.

Printed in the USA
CPSIA information can be obtained
at www.ICGtesting.com
LVHW010301200624
783522LV00009B/743